The Green Movement

Other Books in the Current Controversies Series

Biodiversity

Blogs

Capital Punishment

Darfur

Disaster Response

Drug Trafficking

Espionage and Intelligence

Food

Global Warming

Human Trafficking

Immigration

Online Social Networking

Poverty and Homelessness

Prisons

Racism

Resistant Infections

The U.S. Economy

The World Economy

Violence Against Women

The Green Movement

Debra A. Miller, Book Editor

GREENHAVEN PRESS
A part of Gale, Cengage Learning

GALE
CENGAGE Learning™

Detroit • New York • San Francisco • New Haven, Conn • Waterville, Maine • London

GALE
CENGAGE Learning

Christine Nasso, *Publisher*
Elizabeth Des Chenes, *Managing Editor*

© 2010 Greenhaven Press, a part of Gale, Cengage Learning

Gale and Greenhaven Press are registered trademarks used herein under license.

For more information, contact:
Greenhaven Press
27500 Drake Rd.
Farmington Hills, MI 48331-3535
Or you can visit our Internet site at gale.cengage.com

For product information and technology assistance, contact us at

Gale Customer Support, 1-800-877-4253
For permission to use material from this text or product, submit all requests online at
www.cengage.com/permissions

Further permissions questions can be emailed to permissionrequest@cengage.com

Articles in Greenhaven Press anthologies are often edited for length to meet page require-ments. In addition, original titles of these works are changed to clearly present the main thesis and to explicitly indicate the author's opinion. Every effort is made to ensure that Greenhaven Press accurately reflects the original intent of the authors. Every effort has been made to trace the owners of copyrighted material.

LIBRARY OF CONGRESS CATALOGING-IN-PUBLICATION DATA

The green movement / Debra A. Miller, book editor.
   p. cm. -- (Current controversies)
Includes bibliographical references and index.
ISBN 978-0-7377-4913-7 (hardcover) -- ISBN 978-0-7377-4914-4 (pbk.)
1. Green movement. 2. Environmental responsibility. I. Miller, Debra A.
GE195.G738 2010
333.72--dc22

                                                                        2010003354

Printed in the United States of America
1 2 3 4 5 6 7 14 13 12 11 10

Contents

Foreword   **15**

Introduction   **18**

Chapter 1: Is the Green Movement a Viable Reform Effort?

Chapter Preface   **23**

Yes: The Green Movement Is a Viable Reform Effort

The Green Movement Has   **27**
Developed a Broad Consensus Devoted
to a Sustainable World

Alex Steffen

The environmental movement has moved from the outskirts of activism to the centers of power, as both heads of state and large corporations call for big environmental changes. Green activists must now move from working to create awareness of environmental problems to creating solutions and building a truly sustainable future.

Corporations Will Drive Green Practices   **32**
into the Mainstream

Charles Lockwood

Many companies around the world are going green in their workplaces, operations, products and services, and business and supplier relationships. Some businesses may want to save the environment, but most are motivated by the money they can save. Corporations can therefore be expected to make sustainable practices a standard part of doing business.

**No: The Green Movement Is Not a Viable
Reform Effort**

The Green Economy Has Been   39
Historically Elusive
Joshua Green

The United States was poised to promote green technologies in the 1970s when Jimmy Carter was president, but
succeeding presidents decided to cling to fossil fuels,
causing the U.S. green movement to shrivel. Now we are
once again at a point where interest in green ideas is expanding, but the green movement's success will depend
on whether there is sustained government support that
encourages American entrepreneurial innovations.

The Modern Green Movement Is Divided   49
About How to Address Climate Change
Jeffrey Ball

Faced with the global challenge of climate change, environmentalists are of two mind-sets regarding how to
fight it. Some activists want to continue to back certain
technological fixes on a small scale, while others are calling for banning greenhouse gases completely and letting
industry figure out how to meet the challenge.

The Green Movement Cannot Be   53
Trusted Because It Is Hostile to Science
and Technology
Anthony Giddens

The heart of the green movement is based on a romantic
back-to-nature ideal that is inherently hostile to science
and technology. Climate change is one of the biggest
challenges humans have ever faced, and we will need environmental and energy technologies to deal with it;
therefore, environmentalists should not guide this effort.

**Chapter 2: Will the Green Movement
Benefit the Economy?**

Chapter Preface   58

Yes: The Green Movement Will Benefit the Economy

The Green Business Movement   **61**
Is Taking Off
Michael S. Rosenwald

The green business marketplace is developing rapidly and is being embraced by big companies such as Wal-Mart and General Electric Co. These large companies are helping to establish the movement and expand the market for novel environmental products.

A Green Economy Will Produce Many   **67**
New Green Jobs
John Podesta

A government investment of $100 billion over two years would create 2 million new green jobs, many of them good jobs in struggling blue-collar construction and manufacturing sectors. This type of investment will also help to jump-start a much-needed transformation for our nation from fossil fuels to clean energy.

A Green Economy Could Lift Millions   **72**
Out of Poverty
Preeti Mangala Shekar and Tram Nguyen

Green jobs—many of which will be good manual labor jobs that require little education—could reverse the chronically high rates of unemployment among people of color and lift millions of unemployed, underemployed, or displaced workers out of poverty. The challenge, however, is to create a model for bringing these jobs to marginalized communities.

The Benefits to Green Marketing Are   **81**
More than Hype
Stuart Atkins, MBA

The green movement not only helps the environment, but also makes sense from a purely business point of view. Marketing products that are eco-friendly or use green techniques in areas such as packaging and reduction of wastes can produce real monetary benefits for all types of businesses.

No: The Green Movement Will Not Benefit the Economy

There Are Many Barriers to a   86
Green Economy
Paul Hannam

Making the massive economic transition to a green economy will require training and hiring millions of people for green jobs and will take time, financial investment, and an adjustment of people's expectations. In addition, major barriers including the challenges posed by the recession, talent shortages, problems of greenwashing, and the need for more government regulation stand in the way.

Green Jobs Will Be Too Expensive   92
George Will

The Barack Obama administration wants to emulate Spain's investments in green energy, but a recent report found that the green jobs created in Spain are often temporary and cost the government $752,000 to $800,000 each in subsidies. Creating green jobs for political reasons makes no economic sense.

The Top Green Companies Are Also   95
Major Polluters
Ash Allen

Most of America's largest companies have embraced the green movement, and many of their green initiatives have had a positive impact. The problem, however, is that many of these so-called green companies are also the most excessive polluters in the country.

Re-engineering the World's Energy System   108
Will Be Difficult and Costly
Robert J. Samuelson

Environmentalists typically claim that greening the American economy will cost very little, but weaning industries from fossil fuels is a huge undertaking that will encounter countless difficulties and costs. In truth, no one really knows what the consequences or costs will be.

Chapter 3: Is Going Green Worth the Extra Costs to Consumers?

Chapter Preface   **113**

Yes: Going Green Is Worth the Extra Costs to Consumers

Buying Green Products Pays Off   **116**
in the Long Run
Yumi Araki

The green industry is experiencing a downturn because of the bad economy, but consumers continue to be interested in green products. People understand that buying environmentally sustainable and energy-efficient products, even though they may be more expensive than their non-green counterparts, will save money in the long run.

The Extra Costs of Going Green on   **120**
Consumer Products Are Often Justified
Kimberly Palmer

Green products—such as organic food or personal hygiene and home products—are often more expensive than their mainstream counterparts, but sometimes the extra spending is worth it because of environmental or health benefits. Also, a cheaper green alternative that does not break the budget often exists.

There Are Few Extra Costs and Many   **124**
Lasting Benefits to Green Building Design
Jennifer Crawford and Peter Morris

Green building strategies can directly lead to important environmental benefits. In addition, green buildings can be built with little to no added costs beyond the cost range of non-green buildings and can benefit businesses by providing a cleaner, healthier building with reduced energy and operating costs.

Cap-and-Trade Legislation Will   131
Create Only a Modest Increase in
Homeowners' Energy Costs
      Congressional Budget Office
      Reducing global warming by implementing a cap-and-
      trade program will stem the demand for fossil fuels by
      increasing their price. However, the Congressional Bud-
      get Office estimates that the net annual cost of a cap-
      and-trade program in 2020 would be $22 billion, or only
      about $175 per household.

Cap and Trade Will Be Costly for   138
Consumers, but It Is the Best Option
for Reducing Carbon Emissions
      Neal Dikeman
      To reduce carbon emissions levels, carbon must be priced
      into the economy, an action that will add new costs for
      most industries—costs that ultimately will be passed on
      to consumers. A cap-and-trade program is the fastest,
      least costly, and fairest way to make this transition.

**No: Going Green Is Not Worth the Extra
Costs to Consumers**

Hybrid Cars May or May Not Be Worth   145
the Extra Cost
      Lauren DeAngelis
      Going green on car purchases may or may not be worth
      it, depending on what car the consumer buys. Hybrid
      cars can cost significantly more than gasoline-powered
      models, but some of the green models do not really save
      that much on gas. Similarly, giving up performance or
      space for a conventional car that is more gas-efficient
      may not result in significant yearly gas savings.

Consumers' Costs for Cap-and-Trade   149
Legislation Are Grossly Underestimated
David W. Kreutzer, Karen Campbell,
and Nicolas D. Loris

The Congressional Budget Office's analysis of the costs of
cap-and-trade legislation does not take into account serious economic impacts from the increases in energy price.
Americans will essentially have to pay these costs, but
will get virtually nothing in return.

Cap-and-Trade Legislation Is a   154
Convoluted Scheme to Impose a New
Tax on American Families
David Harsanyi

The cap-and-trade bill under consideration by the U.S.
Congress would impose a substantial tax on American
households and create a complex bureaucratic scheme
susceptible to fraud, insider trading, and political influence. At the same time, it would provide very negligible
environmental benefits.

Chapter 4: What Is the Future for the Green Movement?

Chapter Preface   159

The Green Movement Must Articulate   162
a Vision for a Positive Green Future
Joel Makower

The green movement has painted a clear picture of what
will happen if the world fails to address environmental
problems, but it has failed to create a vision of what happens if we get things right. It's important that environmentalists and President Barack Obama describe a positive image of green to inspire the nation to transform
itself into an environmentally sustainable economy and
society.

African Americans Need to Be Included   168
in the Green Agenda
   John Kerry

   Environmentalism has long been seen as a cause important to white people, but African Americans living in urban areas have the most to lose from pollution and climate change. In the future, the green movement must
   involve everyone in the struggle for a greener environment, including African Americans.

Green Technology Will Create   172
Economic Opportunity
   Associated Press

   Factors such as the rising cost of fuel, economic expansion in China and India, and concerns about global
   warming are likely to fuel investments in green technology. This new sector—which includes technologies related to water purification, air quality, alternative fuels,
   and more—could become as lucrative in the future as information technology and biotechnology are today.

Green-Collar Jobs Are the Future for the   175
Next Generation Workforce
   Wendy Priesnitz

   True "green-collar jobs" work to improve the natural,
   economic, and social environments alike, and the demand for these jobs is expected to increase to support
   sustainable infrastructure amidst a struggling economy.

The U.S. Congress Must Pass   182
Cap-and-Trade Legislation to Move
America into Clean Energy
   Ed Perry

   A cap-and-trade system will make the fossil fuel industry
   pay for polluting the atmosphere and will allow alternative energy industries—such as solar, geothermal, and
   wind power—to compete on a level playing field. Our
   future lies in clean, renewable energy and our legislators
   need to make that happen.

The World Must Figure Out How to   **185**
Mesh Economic Development with Good
Environmental Policies

Anne Applebaum

Rapid economic growth in developing countries will
mean that millions more people will soon be driving cars
and purchasing other consumer goods—a scenario that
points toward an exponential rise in carbon emissions in
the future. Technology may eventually be able to produce
environmentally sustainable development, but first policy
makers need to acknowledge and address these trade-
offs.

A Low-Carbon Economy Will Create   **189**
a Livable Future

Alok Jha

The details of a worldwide low-carbon economy will depend on thousands of decisions by governments, businesses, and individuals about how to balance environmental and economic concerns. It is likely, however, that
the world will look much the same as it does today, but
with changes in the ways electricity is generated, resources are used, and food is produced.

The New Green Movement Will Upgrade   **193**
Our Civilization

Alex Steffen

Unlike earlier environmentalists who failed to mobilize
people because they rejected technology, business, and
prosperity, the new green movement embraces technological solutions, sees business as a vehicle for change,
and thinks green prosperity is possible. Redesigning civilization along green lines will bring a higher quality of
life than most people can imagine.

Organizations to Contact   **197**

Bibliography   **202**

Index   **208**

Foreword

By definition, controversies are "discussions of questions in which opposing opinions clash" (Webster's Twentieth Century Dictionary Unabridged). Few would deny that controversies are a pervasive part of the human condition and exist on virtually every level of human enterprise. Controversies transpire between individuals and among groups, within nations and between nations. Controversies supply the grist necessary for progress by providing challenges and challengers to the status quo. They also create atmospheres where strife and warfare can flourish. A world without controversies would be a peaceful world; but it also would be, by and large, static and prosaic.

The Series' Purpose

The purpose of the Current Controversies series is to explore many of the social, political, and economic controversies dominating the national and international scenes today. Titles selected for inclusion in the series are highly focused and specific. For example, from the larger category of criminal justice, Current Controversies deals with specific topics such as police brutality, gun control, white collar crime, and others. The debates in Current Controversies also are presented in a useful, timeless fashion. Articles and book excerpts included in each title are selected if they contribute valuable, long-range ideas to the overall debate. And wherever possible, current information is enhanced with historical documents and other relevant materials. Thus, while individual titles are current in focus, every effort is made to ensure that they will not become quickly outdated. Books in the Current Controversies series will remain important resources for librarians, teachers, and students for many years.

In addition to keeping the titles focused and specific, great care is taken in the editorial format of each book in the series. Book introductions and chapter prefaces are offered to provide background material for readers. Chapters are organized around several key questions that are answered with diverse opinions representing all points on the political spectrum. Materials in each chapter include opinions in which authors clearly disagree as well as alternative opinions in which authors may agree on a broader issue but disagree on the possible solutions. In this way, the content of each volume in Current Controversies mirrors the mosaic of opinions encountered in society. Readers will quickly realize that there are many viable answers to these complex issues. By questioning each author's conclusions, students and casual readers can begin to develop the critical thinking skills so important to evaluating opinionated material.

Current Controversies is also ideal for controlled research. Each anthology in the series is composed of primary sources taken from a wide gamut of informational categories including periodicals, newspapers, books, U.S. and foreign government documents, and the publications of private and public organizations. Readers will find factual support for reports, debates, and research papers covering all areas of important issues. In addition, an annotated table of contents, an index, a book and periodical bibliography, and a list of organizations to contact are included in each book to expedite further research.

Perhaps more than ever before in history, people are confronted with diverse and contradictory information. During the Persian Gulf War, for example, the public was not only treated to minute-to-minute coverage of the war, it was also inundated with critiques of the coverage and countless analyses of the factors motivating U.S. involvement. Being able to sort through the plethora of opinions accompanying today's major issues, and to draw one's own conclusions, can be a complicated and frustrating struggle. It is the editors' hope that Current Controversies will help readers with this struggle.

Introduction

"Although the 'green' movement seems like a new trend, it actually is rooted in the environmental movement, an appreciation for and effort to protect the natural environment that began early in the country's history."

The concept of "going green" is seen everywhere in American culture these days. Politicians talk about green jobs, television shows focus on green building techniques, and corporations run ads touting their green credentials. Although the "green" movement seems like a new trend, it actually is rooted in the environmental movement, an appreciation for and effort to protect the natural environment that began early in the country's history.

One of the country's earliest champions of nature and the environment was Henry David Thoreau, author of the book *Walden*, an account of a two-year period (1845–47) that Thoreau spent living in relative solitude on the edge of Walden Pond near Concord, Massachusetts. Although he was an independent thinker, Thoreau today is thought of as part of an intellectual movement known as Transcendentalism, which called for the conservation of and respect for nature and for federal preservation of virgin forests. Thoreau and others challenged a common idea of that time—that cultivating and exploiting nature to produce farm products and for other human uses was always the best way to manage property. Thoreau and his supporters believed that preserving lands in their wild state also has great value and is essential to maintaining the proper balance between man and nature.

These early ideas about nature were given form later in the nineteenth century, when the United States government began to set aside large tracts of American wilderness for public parks and preservation. The first region to be declared a national park—in 1872—was Yosemite, a vast wilderness area in northern California's Sierra Nevada mountain range. This achievement was due, in large part, to the activism of John Muir, a Scottish-born American naturalist and author. Muir first visited Yosemite in 1868, and for more than a decade thereafter, he lived in the region, writing letters, essays, and books about his adventures. Muir's advocacy on behalf of nature helped to save not only Yosemite, but also Sequoia National Park and other wilderness areas. In addition, he founded the Sierra Club, one of the oldest and most important environmental organizations in the nation.

It was American president Theodore Roosevelt, however, who popularized Muir's environmental conservation ideas and placed the federal government at the center of efforts to protect the nation's remaining wild areas. At that point in American history, the western frontier was largely settled and the country was just beginning to understand that its supply of land was not unlimited. Forests and soils were being rapidly depleted by farmers and timber industries, and water rights were often managed by private parties with little concern for the environment. Roosevelt, an avid sportsman and naturalist, saw the need for preserving and managing the nation's natural resources and committed his administration to making those changes. One of his first achievements was the Newlands Reclamation Act of 1902, which gave the federal government the power to manage the nation's water resources. Roosevelt's most significant legacy, however, was the preservation of millions of acres of wilderness areas, mostly in the West, in the form of national parks and monuments. In fact, according to the National Geographic Society, the area of the United States placed under public protection by Teddy Roosevelt comes to a total of approximately 230,000,000 acres, or about 84,000 acres each day of his presidency. In 1916, the government established the National Park Service, an agency in the U.S. Department of the Interior, to manage the country's national parks.

Following World War II, which spawned numerous chemical and technological changes in farming and industry, the environmental movement became less concerned with preserving wildlands as national parks and more involved with protecting the environment from toxins and human degradation. One of the key triggers for these new environmental concerns was the writing and advocacy of American scientist and ecologist, Rachel Carson. In 1962, Carson's book, *Silent Spring*, created a worldwide furor by detailing the dangers of agricultural pesticides and calling for new government policies to protect human health and the environment. The book energized a new stage of the U.S. environmental movement that saw the creation of the first Earth Day (1970); the founding of a number of private environmental groups; and the establishment of the U.S. Environmental Protection Agency (1970). In addition, one of the most dangerous pesticides exposed by Rachel Carson—dichlorodiphenyltrichloroethane (DDT)—was banned by the U.S. government for most uses in 1972. Most important, this reengaged environmental effort won the passage of several important pieces of legislation that still form the backbone of the U.S. government's effort to protect and clean up the environment—the Wilderness Act (1964); the National Environmental Policy Act (1969); the Clean Air Act (1970); and the Endangered Species Act (1973).

These new government measures were not enough, however, to prevent a series of environmental disasters in the 1970s and 1980s. There was chemical contamination of a residential development, Love Canal, in New York State in 1978, followed by an accident at a nuclear plant, Three Mile Island, in Pennsylvania in 1979. The 1980s became known for oil spills, such as the *Exxon Valdez*'s disastrous spill in 1989 in Prince William Sound, Alaska. These frightening incidents helped to galvanize a number of radical environmental groups, such as Earth First!, People for the Ethical Treatment of Animals (PETA), and Earth Liberation Front (ELF).

The last couple of decades have witnessed yet another new phase of the environmental movement. Today, environmental advocates are increasingly concerned about a host of even more serious environmental problems—the impact of chemical pesticides, fertilizers, and other chemicals used in agriculture; contamination of soil and fresh water sources; possible shortages of oil and other precious commodities; and of course, worldwide climate change. These issues are also attracting the attention of prominent politicians and policy makers. In 2006, for example, former U.S. vice president Al Gore released a film and a book, both titled *An Inconvenient Truth*, urging the U.S. government to take strong action to stem the carbon emissions that contribute to global warming. President Barack Obama, meanwhile, hopes to revive the U.S. economy with green jobs and a focus on alternative energies, and he has expressed support for legislation that would put a cap on carbon emissions and create an emissions trading program in the United States. Leaders of other countries such as Germany and Spain have made even greater strides toward a green agenda.

Many environmental activists believe that the time has come to do more than simply regulate and limit environmental damage. Instead, activists see the need for a fundamental restructuring of the way the U.S. and world economies function—a green revolution that moves us away from dependence on fossil fuels and their toxic products toward sustainable, environmentally friendly products and practices that rely on organic agriculture and alternative energies such as solar, geothermal, and wind power. This mission is the essence of the new green movement. Only time will tell whether it will succeed.

CHAPTER 1

Is the Green Movement a Viable Reform Effort?

Chapter Preface

Although it seems unlikely, a small town in Kansas is becoming a model for green building and living. Ironically, the town's name is Greensburg—not a new name, but one that has existed since the town's founding in 1886. Greensburg's foray into green development, however, arose out of tragedy. On May 4, 2007, the town was hit by a monster tornado that scored an "F5"—the highest possible rating for a tornado in the United States. The tornado, which was 1.7 miles (2.7 km) wide with winds of more than two hundred miles per hour, ravaged the small community of about 1,574 residents, killed twelve people, and completely destroyed 95 percent of the town's buildings, roads, and infrastructure. Virtually all that was left was rubble, dead tree stumps, sidewalks, and underground sewer lines. Fortunately, tornado sirens sounded in the area twenty minutes before the tornado struck and officials declared a tornado emergency—actions that surely saved many lives.

After the tornado, policy makers and citizens of Greensburg decided to turn tragedy into opportunity by making a historic decision to rebuild the town as a model "green" city. First, the Greensburg city council passed a resolution stating that all city buildings would be built to LEED platinum standards. This is the highest possible rating under the Leadership in Energy and Environmental Design (LEED) Green Building Rating System—standards for environmentally sustainable construction developed by experts from the U.S. Green Building Council. Greensburg is the first city in the nation to do this.

Within two years, the town had completed a number of LEED platinum municipal buildings. One of the first to be finished was a business incubator designed to help area retail businesses rebound after the tornado losses. The incubator was built with $2 million in federal government funding and a $1.1 million donation from Frito-Lay. The town also completed a new city hall, school, hospital, and public housing development—all LEED platinum certified. In addition, Greensburg has broken ground for a kindergarten through twelfth grade school that will be completed in 2010 as a LEED platinum structure, and it has plans for a green county courthouse, library, and arts center. It also hopes to create a new town square and tourism center, and establish a paperless, digital record-keeping system and state-of-the-art wireless communications throughout the community.

The city's energy plan includes projects for power sources such as wind, solar, methane, natural gas, and biofuels, as well as LED street lighting—which is 40 percent more efficient than traditional fixtures and also prevents nighttime light pollution by focusing light downward onto the street. A project involving the installation of ten huge wind turbines will not only produce electricity, it also is expected to generate carbon offsets that the city can sell to companies that need to compensate for their carbon emissions. Reportedly, a number of companies have already pledged to purchase these offsets from Greensburg.

At the same time, Greensburg has urged its citizens to rebuild using green concepts. The leader of this effort is Daniel Wallach, a resident from the Greensburg region who founded Greensburg GreenTown, a nonprofit organization that is helping residents learn about and implement sustainable rebuilding techniques. The group is building a group of twelve Eco-Homes—houses with energy-efficient features that will function as demonstration models to teach people from Greensburg and around the world about energy-efficient, sustainable construction. The first of these to be completed is a silo-shaped building with geothermal heating and cooling and solar hot water, which is designed to be about 70 percent more energy efficient than the average house. It also is made from steel-reinforced concrete and engineered to stand up to future tornadoes. To prove the building's strength, the builder actually used a crane to drop a Ford Escort onto the roof. After two drops, there was no damage to the building, although the car was totaled.

Greensburg citizens and businesses have embraced the green initiative and are constructing houses and buildings that incorporate energy-efficient and tornado-proof designs. One early example is the Greensburg John Deere dealership, a thirty thousand square foot industrial building completed in January 2009 with LEED platinum certification. The metal building incorporates high-value insulation in the walls and roof, uses twenty-four skylights to reduce electricity use, and features a high-efficiency heating, cooling, and ventilation system with a radiant heating system built into the concrete slab floors. Two large wind turbines provide electricity to the facility.

Many of the more than two hundred homes built to replace those that were destroyed in the tornado have also been constructed with sustainable design techniques and advanced energy-efficient equipment. Besides better insulation and more efficient heating, other sustainable building techniques being used in homes include passive solar designs, geothermal heating and cooling systems, and a variety of different wall systems. One popular construction technology uses ICFs (insulating concrete forms) made of Styrofoam. These foam walls are then filled with concrete; and together, the concrete and Styrofoam are not only very strong, but they also act as super-insulators to keep the home warm in the winter and cool in the summer. Other green wall systems include SIPs (structural insulated panels), straw bales, adobe bricks, and advanced frame construction. Despite their incorporation of state-of-the-art green building techniques, however, most green homes have the appearance of typical, traditional homes.

Greensburg's remarkable story has attracted nationwide attention. Television documentaries on the town's reconstruction, for example, have aired on ABC and Planet Green, a sister network to the Discovery Channel. President Barack Obama has publicly commended Greensburg as an inspiring example of how people around the globe can work together to create clean energy and sustainable communities. Greensburg has earned praise for creating a workable vision of how a sustainable world can be achieved. Greensburg city planners have often said that they are not just rebuilding; they are making decisions that will benefit future generations.

The viewpoints in the following chapter address whether efforts such as those in Greensburg—and the green movement in general—are viable in economic and other terms.

The Green Movement Has Developed a Broad Consensus Devoted to a Sustainable World

Alex Steffen

Alex Steffen is the executive editor of Worldchanging.com, a nonprofit Internet organization that champions environmental sustainability.

Al Gore [former vice president] and the IPCC [Intergovernmental Panel on Climate Change, an international scientific body that researches climate change] winning the Nobel Peace Prize symbolizes more than just a head nod towards some eco-fad—it shows that sustainability has finally moved from the outskirts of activism to the most central halls of authority. Concern for the planetary future is now as credible as it is possible to get. The beginning of the struggle to save ourselves from ecological catastrophe has come to an end and we can begin to see the outlines of the next stage of the struggle.

Concern for the planetary future is now as credible as it is possible to get.

Those of us who've spent our careers advocating a saner approach to the future can be forgiven a few moments of smugness, for these are sweet days. There is no longer any reasonable debate about whether or not we need to move with all possible speed towards a different way of living on this planet. To argue the contrary is now to prove oneself morally bankrupt.

Alex Steffen, "Al Gore, the Nobel Prize and the End of the Beginning," Worldchanging .com, October 12, 2007. Reproduced by permission.

Leaders Are Calling for Environmental Changes

Of course, the morally bankrupt can still be found in some numbers in the corridors of commercial and political power, but we don't need to worry too much about them. They are the leaders of the past: Their influence wanes by the moment, as leader after leader steps up to call for big changes.

Consider, for example, German Chancellor Angela Merkel's call this week [October 9, 2007] for a global system of carbon regulation and pricing to be in place by 2012: Merkel insisted that only by establishing limits on carbon dioxide output per individual around the world—suggesting about two tons per head—could the fight to stop global warming be effective.... Her suggestion would mean drastic cuts: Germany has a carbon dioxide output of some 11 tons per person per year, while the U.S. is at around 20 tons per person.

There is no longer any reasonable debate about whether or not we need to move with all possible speed towards a different way of living on this planet.

Similar proclamations—which would, even five years ago, [have] been perceived as beyond the pale of realistic debate—can be heard from corporate CEOs [chief executive officers], retired generals and religious leaders. (These conversions are coming none too soon. There's been a spate of disturbing news of late, including NASA [National Aeronautics and Space Administration] climate expert Jim Hansen's latest paper estimating that we are moving towards an increase of six degrees Celsius rather than three, and that drastic observed effects (like the rapid melting of the polar ice cap) may be evidence that we are on the verge of climate tipping points.

Envisioning the Future

Winning the debate doesn't mean we're winning the war, yet. But the fight has changed. Now that we have an increasingly broad consensus that we face a major planetary crisis, we can start in on the next step. Now we move from spreading the word to setting the agenda, from handing out pamphlets to drawing blueprints. The future we're inheriting is broken. People all over the world know it. Now it's time to design a future that works.

This campaign will be no easier.

For one thing, in order to create real solutions, we have to avoid certain traps, like carbon blindness. It's going to be difficult to help the world see more clearly that climate change is a symptom of our lack of sustainability, not its cause. We must find ways of showing that climate chaos, environmental degradation, economic inequity and political corruption are all part of the same problem. We simply cannot solve any of those problems without working to tackle them all.

Others will call for "moderation," which in this context actually means totally insufficient half-measures. Because we know that we're dealing with the hard reality of merciless trends here, we'll have to be strong and demand more than timid steps and vague pronouncements. We'll have to demand commitment to the bold timelines necessary and hold our leaders accountable to them. To take baby steps now is to fail, however good our intentions.

We'll have to demand commitment to the bold timelines necessary and hold our leaders accountable to them. To take baby steps now is to fail, however good our intentions.

We'll also have some work to do explaining why the developed world needs to lead the way. We in the North have a moral responsibility to go first, of course, both because we bear the historical guilt for the situation in which we find ourselves and because others have the same right we do to expect reasonable prosperity and we will not earn their cooperation (which we need) without acknowledging that. But we also face the practical reality that it is our governments, universities and businesses that have the research capacity to forge the new solutions people everywhere will need. If we want the whole world using these new solutions by 2050, we'd better start inventing and implementing them here, now.

Massive Changes Are Ahead

But there's an even more fundamental challenge facing us, I believe: We don't know what the future we want to build looks like.

We are coming to understand the kinds of radical challenges we face—cutting our impact on the planet by perhaps a factor of 20 over the next 25 years or so, while delivering sustainable prosperity to many more people—but the truth we rarely speak in public is that we really have no idea how to get there.

We don't know what our cities will look like, how our energy will be created and delivered, how we'll get from place to place, how our food will be grown, how we'll manufacture our consumer products and make our clothing, or even how we'll recreate and relax. Yet we will need revolutions in each of these fields—and in the cultural interactions between them, the policies regulating them, and in the businesses which deliver them.

Up to now, we have been a movement whose purpose was to raise awareness of the dangers of a broken future; education and persuasion will continue to be part of our job, but now our central mission must evolve into creating a networked movement of people and institutions who are working together to imagine, describe, plan and build a sustainable society. We have shown people the need for change; now we need to become capable of mass producing it. Our business now is vision.

It's common, among certain of our allies, to try to avoid seeming like radicals by reassuring people that a sustainable world won't be all that different from the world we live in now. It's time for us to stop saying that.

It's time for us to stop saying that because it's not true: The kind of world we will be building will have to include what are, from today's perspective, some truly massive changes. We won't be living the same way in a couple decades, either because we've undergone some relatively profound transformations, or because the consequences of failing to change our ways will be coming home to roost in a series of utterly predictable disasters.

Now our central mission must ... [be] to imagine, describe, plan and build a sustainable society.

But it's time to stop downplaying the changes needed for another reason: If we do our jobs right, life will get better. The systems we currently rely on don't just destroy the environment, they limit our happiness. We do not live in the best of all possible worlds. We know it is possible to create lives that are not only profoundly more sustainable, but more prosperous, comfortable, stylish, healthy, safe and fun. If we do our jobs right, a bright green future will be downright *sexy*.

Our task now is to envision those lives, envision them with such practical clarity that we gain the power to build them.

Getting to a bright green future is going to involve quite a long journey. The storms of bad news won't stop coming in the meantime, and we can expect the seas to be choppy along the way. But this will also be a grand adventure and we can take heart in the message the Nobel committee has sent: Look to your sails, the tide has turned.

Corporations Will Drive Green Practices into the Mainstream

Charles Lockwood

Charles Lockwood is an environmental and real estate consultant, based in Southern California and New York City.

While businesses may be tempted to adopt environmentally friendly practices for benevolent reasons—sustaining the environment, promoting community goodwill—the big incentive is the extra green it puts in their wallets.

Money talks . . . especially in business.

If a new strategy, product, or technology boosts profitability, companies not only sit up and take notice; they embrace it with open arms.

That's why more and more U.S. and international companies are going green in their workplaces, their day-to-day operations, their products and services, and their business and supplier relationships.

"Going green is no longer just about protecting the environment or even providing a healthier and more productive workplace for employees," says Peter J. Miscovich, a principal within Deloitte Consulting LLP. "Green is also about improving the bottom line. Thus, corporations will drive sustainable practices into the mainstream, yielding tremendous environmental and social benefits while generating increased corporate profits and shareholder value."

Every company that adopts green policies becomes a change agent, because those policies affect and educate everyone who comes into contact with that firm—employees, suppliers, technology providers, clients and customers. People

Charles Lockwood, "The Growth of Green Business," *Hemispheres*, December, 2006. Reproduced by permission of author.

touched by that green-focused company will, in turn, carry their newfound knowledge about sustainability into their private lives, workplaces, and communities.

Going green is no longer just about protecting the environment. . . . Green is also about improving the bottom line.

Green Workplaces

An increasing number of companies are choosing green workplaces because they provide such bottom-line benefits as higher workforce productivity, greater attraction and retention of skilled workers, and lower overhead costs, including electric and heating and air conditioning bills.

Citigroup owns and leases more than 13,000 properties in more than 100 countries. The company has committed to reducing greenhouse gas emissions from its buildings by 10 percent by 2011. Citigroup also is investigating what levels of renovation are necessary to earn Energy Star [a program that sets standards for energy-efficient products] and LEED (Leadership in Energy and Environmental Design) ratings for its existing buildings in the United States, and it has established a LEED silver rating as a target for its new office and operation center facilities worldwide.

Citigroup has 300,000 employees around the world. "Our experience is that employees care tremendously about green issues," says Pamela Flaherty, senior executive vice president of Citigroup's global community relations.

"The way they see that a company is serious about caring for the environment is through their workplace. They may know about the company's other green policies, but those policies are not part of employees' everyday lives. When they see the company implementing green policies in their workplace, however, they know the company is serious about its commitment.

"Young people in particular are very interested in a company's corporate citizenship and environmental responsibilities," Flaherty continues. "We've also seen that many of our younger bankers are interested in working with clients on green issues. Thus, green has become a huge recruiting tool for attracting the best and brightest people."

An increasing number of companies are choosing green workplaces because they provide such bottom-line benefits as higher workforce productivity . . . and lower overhead costs.

Corporate headquarters have gotten the most media coverage, but sustainability is applicable beyond white-collar workplaces. These policies benefit a variety of blue-collar workplaces, too.

Toyota Logistics Services' new 85-acre Port of Portland vehicle distribution center in Portland, Oregon—which serves the company's import vehicle processing and logistics functions—has earned a U.S. Green Building Council LEED gold rating for sustainability.

"We integrated a wide variety of green design, materials, and technologies into every aspect of the buildings and site," says Bob Bonney, the executive vice president of MNB Architects/Engineers of Portland, which designed the project.

The vehicle distribution center features a 6.7-acre riverfront greenway, Energy Star roofs, natural daylighting and outdoor views for 96 percent of the buildings' interior space, and occupancy sensors, which automatically turn off lights in unoccupied spaces. "We used green building materials like zero-VOC [volatile organic compound] composite wood and low-VOC adhesives, sealants, paints, and carpet that don't off-gas toxins like standard building materials do," Bonney says.

Day-to-Day Operations

As companies embrace the benefits of green buildings, they're discovering that sustainable business practices in their daily operations bring many additional benefits: a stronger bottom line, a more satisfied workforce, and greater community goodwill.

India-based Taj Hotels, which has more than 50 luxury hotels and resorts around the world, has instituted a corporate environmental policy—Eco Taj—that addresses many aspects such as conserving energy and water, purchasing eco-products, and minimizing waste.

Corporate headquarters have gotten the most media coverage, but sustainability . . . policies benefit a variety of blue-collar workplaces, too.

In London, Taj's 51 Buckingham Gate hotel near Buckingham Palace has reduced energy consumption by more than 22 percent, cut natural gas consumption by more than 32 percent, and lowered water usage and costs by 25 percent since 2005. The hotel also recycles a variety of materials, including coat hangers, paper and cardboard, glass, and food containers.

"We don't buy anything that comes in plastic," says resident manager Paul Brackley. "Plastic gives off toxic fumes, and it's awful for landfill. We look for everything that can be recycled, and we look for relationships with suppliers that can buy into our policies."

Wal-Mart, the largest retailer in the world, is adopting green practices, which will have a significant impact globally. Its year-old, experimental green supercenters outside Dallas and Denver, for example, are testing a wide variety of sustainable design strategies, materials, and technologies for use in new and existing stores around the world. Wal-Mart plans to increase its fleet efficiency by 25 percent over the next three years and double it within 10 years. It is investing $500 million annually in technologies that will reduce greenhouse gases at existing stores by 20 percent over the next seven years.

Wal-Mart's long-term environmental goals are to use 100 percent renewable energy, to create zero waste, and to sell products that sustain natural resources and the environment. "We are a large company," CEO [chief executive officer] [H.] Lee Scott said in his October 2005 "Twenty First Century Leadership" presentation to employees.

"For Wal-Mart to be successful and continue to grow, we must operate in a world that is healthy and successful."

Products and Technologies

Around the world, farsighted companies are creating new green products and technologies. "Green is going to be the industry of the 21st century," says Thomas L. Friedman, the influential *New York Times* columnist and author of the best-selling book *The World Is Flat*.

As companies reap the many benefits of green . . . they begin insisting that suppliers and business partners adopt green policies, too.

United Technologies Corporation (UTC) certainly agrees. The company's hydrofuel-cell bus, for example, helps to reduce air pollution and a municipality's energy costs, and it educates those who use or see the buses about the practicality of alternative-fuel vehicles.

UTC also is developing technologies that reduce a building's energy consumption and costs. UTC's Otis Gen2 elevators, for example, not only use 70 percent less energy than comparable models ten years ago, but also generate energy that can be used to power building systems, a significant benefit for building owners and the environment.

The European Union is rapidly upgrading its environmental standards, creating many new opportunities for companies. Finland's Proventia Group and its subsidiaries produce machines that cut, separate, and recycle reusable components in television sets and computer monitors, such as leaded and unleaded glass.

With the mainstreaming of green buildings, other companies are creating—and profiting from—the growing market demand for reasonably priced, environmentally responsible construction materials. Chinese companies have developed porous pavement bricks that allow rainwater to percolate down through the pavement into the ground and underground aquifers, thereby replenishing water supplies while reducing stormwater runoff and the threat of flooding.

Dow BioProducts (a subsidiary of the Dow Chemical Company) manufactures strawboard (rather than formaldehyde-laced particle board) that can be used for cupboards and desks. BioBased Insulation of Rogers, Arkansas, has created an effective soybean-based foam insulation to replace standard chemical-laden insulation.

Australia's TecEco Pty. Ltd. has created Eco-Cement, made of reactive magnesia and industrial by-products and requiring lower temperatures and less energy to produce than standard cement. Equally impressive, although standard concrete generates about 10 percent of the world's carbon dioxide emissions, Eco-Cement absorbs (sequesters) carbon dioxide.

Business and Supplier Relationships

As companies reap the many benefits of green, something interesting happens. They begin insisting that suppliers and business partners adopt green policies, too.

Wal-Mart is creating a program that gives preference to suppliers who aggressively reduce their greenhouse gas emissions. Wal-Mart also is working with its suppliers to create less packaging overall, increase the recycling of packaging, and increase the use of recycled materials.

Bank of America is acting as a green agent in many ways. Its Bank of America Tower, now under construction in Manhattan, is on target to earn a LEED platinum rating. That effort affects every professional, contractor, and supplier on the project. Bank of America requires its hundreds of vendors to comply with its environmental standards. All paper suppliers must provide independent, third-party certification of their sustainable forestry practices for all forests they own or manage. In addition, Bank of America reduced its paper usage by 32 percent between 2000 and 2005, even though its customer base grew by 24 percent. "We are also recycling 30,000 tons of paper a year," says Mark Nicholls, senior vice president of Bank of America's corporate workplace.

Leading corporations are forming organizations with strong sustainable goals. More than 180 international companies have joined the World Business Council for Sustainable Development based in Geneva, Switzerland, an organization committed to environmentally responsible economic growth. One current council initiative will identify practical strategies to construct buildings that consume "zero net energy."

The three Ps—people, profits, and the planet—will all benefit from this worldwide change in corporate attitudes about sustainability and the environment.

"I think that over the next five to 10 years, green practices will become embedded in how companies conduct all of their business," says Citigroup's Flaherty. "Green practices will be the standard way that we address the environmental and human impact of building development and renovation and the standard way we interact with our clients, our employees, and our suppliers."

That optimism may be the best evidence that the growth of green policies is rooted in a burgeoning bottom line.

The Green Economy Has Been Historically Elusive

Joshua Green

Joshua Green is a senior editor of the Atlantic, *an American magazine that focuses on politics, foreign affairs, and the economy.*

In October 1977, this magazine [the *Atlantic*] ran a cover story on the promising field of renewable energy. From today's vantage point, the article is noteworthy mainly for how uncannily its description of the country's energy crisis and possible solutions applies to the crisis we're in now.

The article took as its starting point the national debate that had arisen over a 29-year-old physicist named Amory Lovins, who had come to prominence a year earlier, when he published an essay in *Foreign Affairs* called "Energy Strategy: The Road Not Taken?" Lovins argued that the country had arrived at an important crossroads and could take one of two paths. The first, supported by U.S. policy at the time, promised a future of steadily increasing reliance on dirty fossil fuels and nuclear fission, and it carried serious environmental risks. At a time before [former vice president] Al Gore was even in Congress, Lovins noted: "The commitment to a long-term coal economy many times the scale of today's makes the doubling of atmospheric carbon dioxide concentration early in the next century virtually unavoidable, with the prospect then or soon thereafter of substantial and perhaps irreversible changes in global climate." He dubbed this "the hard path."

The alternative, which Lovins called "the soft path," favored "benign" sources of renewable power like wind and the sun, along with a heightened commitment to meeting energy demands through conservation and efficiency. Such a hetero-dox blend of clean technologies, Lovins argued, would bring a host of salutary effects: a healthier environment, an end to our dependence on Middle East oil, a diminished likelihood of future wars over energy, and the foundation of a vibrant new economy.

In 1977, the country appeared poised on the brink of a new age, with . . . a clean-energy future . . . tantalizingly close at hand.

The *Atlantic* cover story went on to examine emerging technologies, like solar energy, that lay at the heart of Lovins's vision. While refraining from outright prediction, the author's hopes were clear. In 1977, the country appeared poised on the brink of a new age, with recent events having organized them-selves in such a way as to make a clean-energy future seem tantalizingly close at hand. A charismatic Democrat had come from nowhere to win the White House. Reacting to an oil shock and determined to rid the country of Middle East en-tanglements, he was touting the merits of renewable energy and, for the first time, putting real money into it—$368 mil-lion.

But things peaked soon afterward, when Jimmy Carter in-stalled solar panels on the roof of the White House. "A gen-eration from now," Carter declared, "this solar heater can ei-ther be a curiosity, a museum piece, an example of a road not taken—or it can be a small part of one of the greatest and most exciting adventures ever undertaken by the American people; harnessing the power of the sun to enrich our lives as we move away from our crippling dependence on foreign oil."

Now we have our answer: museum piece. In one of the great acts of humiliating political symbolism, Ronald Reagan tore down the solar panels, which spent many years in purga-tory before eventually finding their way to the Jimmy Carter

Library and Museum in Atlanta, where they sit on display in silent reproach to all who drive HUMMERs and own high-wattage plasma television sets.

A New Awakening?

But having mostly followed the hard path since 1977, the world has started to register the dire climatic effects Lovins warned of. The concentration of atmospheric carbon, an important indicator of global warming, has shot from 280 parts per million [ppm] in pre-industrial times to 386 ppm last year [2008] and appears to be accelerating. Most scientists agree that beyond some critical threshold, climate change is irreversible and probably catastrophic. But no one knows just where the threshold lies. The Intergovernmental Panel on Climate Change [IPCC] takes 450 ppm as the benchmark, a level we're on pace to reach by mid-century—although the prognosis is grimmer than that would imply. Because the effects of atmospheric carbon take years to show up as higher temperatures, limiting concentration to 450 ppm requires halting emissions at current levels. This sudden imperative, coupled with the unlikelihood of action absent a major government intervention, has thrust national energy policy to the forefront of public debate for the first time since Lovins's heyday.

Having mostly followed the hard path since 1977, the world has started to register . . . dire climatic effects.

At least on a rhetorical level, a good portion of the country now seems eager to commit to the soft path. It probably helps that the last administration [President George W. Bush] was synonymous with oil and coal. But last summer's spike in oil prices gave a nudge even to some who harbored [former vice president Dick] Cheney-esque views of renewable energy.

The recent changes in Washington have made a significant shift in the nation's energy policy a real possibility for the first time in years.

As before, a new Democratic president [Barack Obama] is touting clean energy, not only as the path to the future but as the key to economic revival. "To truly transform our economy, protect our security, and save our planet from the ravages of climate change," President Obama told Congress in February, "we need to ultimately make clean, renewable energy the profitable kind of energy." Like Carter, he's putting federal money into the effort, but in an amount several orders of magnitude greater. The stimulus alone dumped $167 billion in grants and loan guarantees for clean energy and other projects onto the Department of Energy, dwarfing its $27 billion annual budget to such a degree that its inspector general frantically warned that the department could buckle under the strain. There's even talk of refitting the White House with solar panels. In all sorts of ways, it feels like 1977 again.

The recent changes in Washington have made a significant shift in the nation's energy policy a real possibility for the first time in years.

Shortly after the inauguration, a friend up for several jobs in the new administration confessed that he yearned to wind up at the Department of Energy. "It's like NASA [National Aeronautics and Space Administration] in the '60s," he told me. "All the best and brightest want to be there." Obama's choice of Steven Chu, the Nobel laureate physicist, as secretary of energy only heightened the allure. In the early Obama era, romantic notions about making one's mark on history tend to take the form of helping recast America's economy, and by extension the world's, in a way that will head off global catastrophe. So we're back at the old crossroads, only with less time and more urgency to act. . . .

The Obama Plan

When Obama took office, the climate change issue had a short-term and a long-term component. The immediate imperative was to find a way of rescuing the renewables industry from Wall Street's collapse. This was important not just as a means of mitigating the recession, but also because getting clean technology rapidly to scale is probably the only way to meet the larger goal of reducing carbon emissions enough to limit climate change. Another setback could make the difficult impossible.

We're back at the old crossroads, only with less time and more urgency to act.

The stimulus was the first of three major initiatives intended to steer the economy toward something more like Amory Lovins's soft path. To fill the tax-equity gap, the stimulus provides $32.7 billion in direct grants and another $134 billion in loan guarantees to attract new investors to large projects. To impose stability, it extends a variety of tax credits by anywhere from three to eight years. Most striking of all, it instructs the Department of Energy to invest directly in promising cleantech companies (though the payoff comes in jobs and environmental gains, not equity). By a stroke of his pen, President Obama made a federal agency the world's largest venture capitalist. When the official in charge of the program appeared at a Santa Barbara energy conference in March, he was mobbed by eager CEOs.

So far, so good. "The stimulus package essentially saved the renewable energy industry in the United States," says Raj Atluru, managing director of the venture-capital firm Draper Fisher Jurvetson.

The second part of the Obama plan, which Congress will consider as part of the energy bill this summer, is to make renewable energy standards, like those already in place in Texas, California, and other states, national policy. This would put the force of law behind the effort to advance clean energy, and eliminate the possibility of another Reagan-esque reversal of course. The final and most significant component, also part of the energy bill, will be putting a price on carbon emissions, possibly by establishing a cap-and-trade system like the one featured in Obama's budget.

All of this could be achieved and still fail to stop climate change—we won't know for years. Beyond a broad consensus on the urgency of the threat, the inability to know precisely what can contain it has produced a range of expert opinions, from optimists convinced that steady government support of existing technology will suffice, to pessimists (they'd say "realists") who consider such support a necessary precondition, to which a great deal more will have to be added. Nathan Lewis, for instance, an energy chemist at the California Institute of Technology, foresees the need to develop 13,000 gigawatts of carbon-free power if we're to limit atmospheric carbon concentration to 450 ppm. (Current global solar power production is 10 gigawatts.) And it will need to be cheap enough to persuade major polluters like China and India to go along. Steven Chu believes this will require "Nobel-caliber" scientific breakthroughs.

Everyone agrees on the need for the sustained focus missing from every earlier attempt to go green. But if that's not enough, then the important question becomes: Where is a Nobel-caliber breakthrough most likely to be made and what might be done to bring it about?

Encouraging Technological Advances

The U.S. record on renewable energy provokes a kind of sheepish embarrassment among many veteran adherents. The mid-1980s collapse brought down not just the domestic industry, but many of the major foreign companies that had invested here. "You can certainly make the case that the policy the U.S. has followed over the last 30 years is exactly the policy you would *not* want to follow," Randy Swisher, the former director of the American Wind Energy Association, told me. Thus the tendency is to regard Carter as a naive optimist and the years between his presidency and *An Inconvenient Truth* [former vice president Al Gore's book and film on global warming] as a kind of Dark Ages best forgotten.

Europe offers a model of how governments can lead the transition to clean energy and thereby reduce demand for fossil fuels.

But Carter's efforts can also be viewed as a qualified but important success. Despite its epic travails, the United States in the mid-1980s was the overwhelming leader in clean technology, with more than 80 percent of the world's wind capacity and 90 percent of solar. The entrepreneurial culture of California in particular drew the best minds from around the world. One of them, Arnold Goldman, was already building toward scale when it all came apart.

The United States has fallen back dramatically since then, both in a moral and an economic sense. As awareness of the climate threat has taken hold, we've drawn contempt, as much for President Bush's truculent dismissal of the Kyoto Protocol [an international environmental treaty that aims to stabilize greenhouse gas concentrations in the atmosphere] as for the amount of greenhouse gases we emit. Even President Obama's sharp change of course seems likely to win us, at best, a prodigal son's wary reception when representatives of 170 nations meet in Copenhagen in December to negotiate the next climate treaty. Meanwhile, the benefits of the developments that emerged in the 1980s have mostly accrued to others. "We sent the wind and solar industry to Europe for three decades," Raj

Atluru says. "As a result, they have both a huge consumption market for renewable energy and the biggest companies that export the technology."

Europe offers a model of how governments can lead the transition to clean energy and thereby reduce demand for fossil fuels. Denmark, which also suffered the shocks of the 1970s, no longer needs to import oil. But missing from Europe's decades of leadership are big breakthroughs in creating renewable energy. The lack of an entrepreneurial culture is a big reason, and it is also why, despite commendable progress, Europe shouldn't be counted on to play the role of savior in the event that Scandinavian practicality alone can't do the job. As an indicator of where a solution might emerge instead, venture-capital investments in clean technology last year reached $5.8 billion in the United States, compared with $1.8 billion in all of Europe and Israel. And that was before Obama's enormous ante.

American capitalism—even when it's working—is not without its limitations, one being that promising ideas rarely get funding if their commercial potential lies beyond venture capitalists' 10-year investment horizon. The Energy Department research budget has never recovered from Reagan's cuts. And the private industry that would seem to have the most at stake in finding and controlling clean-energy advances—electric utilities—has never seriously pursued them, since a century of government policy has made the hard path so easy. People in cleantech circles often point out that the electric utilities spend a smaller portion of revenue on research and development than pet food companies do. Here, too, the stimulus fills a gap. For years, Silicon Valley [a region in California known for its high-tech discoveries and advances] dreamed that government would cultivate nascent but potentially transformative energy ideas by creating an equivalent of the Pentagon's famous Defense Advanced Research Projects Agency (DARPA), which pioneered such things as the Internet and GPS [global positioning system]. With an eye toward similar breakthroughs, the stimulus allots $400 million to the Department of Energy for just such an agency.

The interplay of technology, policy, and finance has always determined the rate at which clean technologies advance.

But the Internet came to fruition only after the right conditions were in place. Its rapid growth and innovation followed from the telecommunications reforms of the 1990s, a consequence few predicted at the time. "The trouble with projections is that they extrapolate from the current reality, and often end up undershooting the mark," Sunil Paul, a founding partner of Spring Ventures, a firm that invests in cleantech, told me. "Over the long haul, dramatic things happen to change the equation. As I like to put it, the history of our future is filled with moon bases, jet packs, and 200-mph cars, but has no cell phones, no Internet, and no laptop computers."

The interplay of technology, policy, and finance has always determined the rate at which clean technologies advance. Today these are aligned for the first time since Jimmy Carter—and more strongly now because the environmental imperative and global concern are so much greater than they were in 1977.

The key to our energy future lies in exploiting two often opposing forces without having them trample or undermine each other: Silicon Valley's free-market culture of innovation and Washington's power to set the terms by which everyone operates. The challenge will be to establish European-style stability without constraining ourselves to anemic European levels of innovation. And if it turns out that a Nobel-caliber breakthrough is necessary to save the planet, the freewheeling boom-and-bust disruptions of the 1980s might come to be regarded in a much better light—because, really, who else has produced such rapid change? It may seem strange to think so, but the last, best hope for heading off climate change is probably the same country that botched the job so badly once before.

The Modern Green Movement Is Divided About How to Address Climate Change

Jeffrey Ball

Jeffrey Ball is a journalist who covers energy and environmental issues for the Wall Street Journal, *an American business newspaper.*

The modern environmental movement is having an identity crisis. Staring down its biggest enemy yet, it's fiercely divided over how to beat it.

The global challenge of climate change is tougher than the localized problems the green movement has spent decades fighting. To some environmentalists, it requires chucking old orthodoxies and getting practical. To others, it demands an old-style moral crusade.

The global challenge of climate change is tougher than the localized problems the green movement has spent decades fighting.

The pragmatists have the upper hand. One sign is that the movement is moving beyond small-scale backyard wind turbines and rooftop solar panels. It's calling for technological change at industrial speed and scale—sometimes to the detriment of local ecologies.

In Europe, environmental groups are backing proposals for massive collections of wind turbines off the continent's Atlantic coast that would amount to seaborne power plants. In California, they're endorsing huge solar panel installations on farmland and in the desert. In Washington, they're lobbying for more spending to develop "clean coal," resigned to the conclusion that scrubbing coal is more plausible than killing it.

"There's a kind of reality check," says Stephan Singer, the Brussels-based director of global energy policy for WWF, an environmental group also called the World Wildlife Fund. The only clean-energy options likely to matter are "large, centralized solutions," he says. "That's the way it is."

Karen Douglas feels the pressure from both sides of the divide. She has spent her career as a green activist in California, and her success has helped move her from outside agitator to inside policy maker. After California passed a law curbing greenhouse gas emissions, Gov. Arnold Schwarzenegger tapped Ms. Douglas early last year to join the California Energy Commission, which has to help figure out how to comply with the law. Recently, she was named chairman.

[Pragmatists in the green movement are] calling for technological change at industrial speed and scale—sometimes to the detriment of local ecologies.

The commission is trying to figure out where big new solar energy installations and electric transmission lines should go. The process is pitting locally oriented environmentalists, whose priority still is to protect California's wilderness, against globally oriented environmentalists whose focus is to get big renewable energy projects built. "I am in an interesting spot," she says. "It's hard."

Mr. Singer of the WWF is in a similar fix. In Europe, the prospect of large-scale renewable energy means the construction of hundreds of wind turbines off the coast. His organization "strongly supports" that move, he says, despite opposition from some local environmentalists who contend such installations might harm birds or fish.

"We all grew up with this kind of mantra that small is beautiful," he says. But that "is not a model for a highly modernized, global world."

Nothing underscores the green movement's soul-searching more than its conflicted view of coal, which provides about half the world's electricity. Should society pour billions of dollars into trying to perfect a way to turn coal into electricity without emitting greenhouse gases? Or should it reject coal as inalterably dirty and try to replace it entirely with renewable sources like the wind and sun?

Late last year, the influential Natural Resources Defense Council [NRDC] helped sponsor ads ridiculing coal industry ads boasting about progress toward cleaning up coal. "In reality, there's no such thing as clean coal," said a print version of the ad.

Rather than push certain technological fixes, critics say, environmentalists should simply push government to slap industry with a tough cap on greenhouse gases.

But last month, the NRDC, along with the Environmental Defense Fund, another prominent group, hosted workshops advocating more spending on clean-coal research. The rationale: Coal will remain a crucial fuel for decades, so it makes sense to try to clean it up.

"If NRDC had written all the ads by itself, we probably would have had a more nuanced ad," says NRDC climate expert David Hawkins. "But it probably would have been a nuanced ad that doesn't get noticed."

Industry claims that coal already is clean are "misleading," says Mr. Hawkins. Still, the technology to generate electricity from coal and capture the carbon dioxide emissions "is both needed and feasible," he says. That was the point of the workshops, he says: that government should implement policies to deploy the technology.

Now, a backlash is building within the movement. Rather than push certain technological fixes, critics say, environmentalists should simply push government to slap industry with a tough cap on greenhouse gases—and let industry figure out how to meet the mandate.

"It's like we're pushing to invent a better cotton gin as a way to reduce slaveholding instead of just banning slaveholding," says the Environmental Defense Fund's John DeCicco. "The environmental movement has become insiders. Is that actually to our benefit now? Or is that to our detriment?"

The Green Movement Cannot Be Trusted Because It Is Hostile to Science and Technology

Anthony Giddens

Anthony Giddens is a British sociologist and author.

It is time to take the issue of climate change out of the hands of the greens. Climate change has suddenly come right to the forefront of public consciousness in the most extraordinary way. You can't open a newspaper without reading about it. The *Stern Report* [a 2006 report by British economist Nicholas (Nick) Stern on climate change] has received mass coverage. Politicians have been scrabbling to respond and to do more than mouth the pious truisms until recently they were able to get away with. Why ditch the green movement just at the moment climate change for the first time is becoming an urgent and widely accepted part of the political agenda? Isn't such an idea, to say the least, ungrateful, given the part that the greens have played in alerting the issue in public consciousness? Shouldn't we all instead become Friends of the Earth?

The Problem with the Green Movement

Actually, it wasn't the green movement that alerted us to the dangers of climate change, it was scientists. Large sectors of the green movement actually have their origins in a quite different body of thinking. They are to be found in the writings of those hostile to modern industry, which was seen as destroying the integrity of nature—essentially a romantic, conservative reaction to industrialism. This threat explains why so many greens are either hostile to science and technology, or at least ambivalent about them. The green movement developed around the idea of the conservation of nature in the face of the advance of human technology. The very imagery of "green"—a return to nature freed as far as possible from human tampering—is wrong. There can be no going back to "nature", since "nature" no longer exists, at least so far as climate is concerned—we are living in a world in which human influence is everywhere. Science and technology have to be a large part of our responses to climate change.

Science and technology have to be a large part of our responses to climate change.

Moreover, the greens function essentially as a special interest group, or cluster of interest groups. Friends of the Earth or Greenpeace are unelected NGOs [nongovernmental organisations], much along the same lines of Oxfam [International], Save the Children and a host of other such organisations. Green parties have rarely got more than 5% of the vote, precisely because they campaign on the basis of a single, overriding set of concerns. Finally, because the green movement grew out of a romantic critique of modernity, it has always been linked to the idea of setting limits, of cutting back, a sort of hair-shirt philosophy of everyday life.

I have in front of me an article written by one of the most prominent British environmentalists, entitled "How Sport Is Killing the Planet." Motor racing, that author says, is simply incompatible with reducing climate change and hence, he implies, should be abandoned. The Olympic Games, involving as they do the building of stadia and a good deal of air travel, should be closed down in their current form. We should encourage spectators to stay at home and watch major sports events on the TV. The best and most involving sport—he seems to say this in all seriousness—is playing in the local park with a Frisbee.

The Full Weight of Human Ingenuity Is Needed

It is therefore a welcome innovation to have a serious and detailed report on climate change produced by a mainstream economist. Nick Stern is a scholar of impeccable reputation and certainly no scaremonger. Since economic considerations are the main reason why there is so much foot-dragging in taking action against climate change, his emphasis upon the sheer economic costs of a failure to respond has a great deal of force. He is right to emphasise carbon pricing, technology and energy efficiency as the three core emphases of future policy.

Environmental technologies are likely to be for the next 20 years what information technology has been for the last 20—a driving force of ... economic and social change.

The normalisation of climate change policy is crucial at this point. Stern emphasises the international dimension, but that of orthodox domestic politics is certainly equally important. Environmental issues for the first time have to be brought within the framework of rights and obligations that constitute the citizenship contract between government and citizens, including both the fiscal and welfare systems. The guiding principle should be that the environment can no longer be treated as a free good.

I do not believe that self-denial should be the key basis of this shift. Rather environmental principles should be integrated with the responsibilities and obligations of citizenship. I'm not saying we can have it all, because we can't. Draconian measures will be needed in some areas, such as control of vehicle pollution, and these will be politically problematic. Tax incentives and tax credits should wherever possible be the motivating factors of lifestyle change, for citizens, public organisations and business firms.

Lifestyle change is central to many areas of politics today, not only to climate change. Health is a good example since, in the developed world, infectious diseases are no longer the main source of illness and death—diet, smoking, lack of exercise—and environmental pollution—are much more central. Fiscal incentives and sanctions, together with education and a sense of personal responsibility, can help to promote positive changes in everyday behaviour—as has been shown by countries, such as Finland, that have turned around their health indicators.

That now forgotten thinker, Karl Marx, said "human beings only set themselves such problems as they can resolve". Well, climate change will be the biggest test of that principle yet. I don't believe Marx's idea is a metaphysical one. It means that when there is an acute enough sense of a crisis, the full weight of human ingenuity tends to be brought into play to resolve it. On that ground I believe there will be major breakthroughs in energy technologies as the pressure for innovation builds. Environmental technologies are likely to be for the next 20 years what information technology has been for the last 20—a driving force of wider economic and social change.

Back to motor racing. I'm not a fan of the sport and hold no particular brief for it. Yet the technology developed in motor sport has contributed perhaps more than any other single factor to the increased fuel efficiency (and safety) of everyday cars. The process of technological advance is oblique and complex.

CHAPTER 2

Will the Green Movement Benefit the Economy?

Chapter Preface

Some of the nation's most prominent corporations have embraced the green movement, among them Wal-Mart, the country's biggest corporation and the largest retailer in the world. Wal-Mart began its green program in 2006, when H. Lee Scott, the company's chief executive officer, announced a sweeping sustainability initiative. As part of the program, the company pledged to cut its energy use by 30 percent and to cut greenhouse gas emissions by 20 percent in seven years. Wal-Mart also intends to reduce solid waste produced by its U.S. stores by 25 percent and to make its trucking fleet more efficient.

Since 2006, Wal-Mart has made numerous changes in its approximately seven thousand stores to make them more energy efficient. The company is installing skylights and replacing lights with energy-saving lightbulbs to reduce its electricity usage; cash register receipts are being printed on both sides of the paper to cut back on the company's paper consumption; and low-flow toilets are being installed to save water. Another important energy-saving change involves fitting freezer cases with motion detectors that turn the lights on only when customers approach.

Wal-Mart is also making other moves toward a more sustainable business operation. Perhaps most significant is a decision to judge its suppliers not just on traditional factors such as price and quality, but also on a new standard—the environmental sustainability of packaging and shipping practices. This program was implemented in 2008 and, according to Wal-Mart executives, has already produced important new green innovations in packaging. Some reports say that Wal-Mart suppliers have reduced the amount of plastic and other packaging by up to 50 percent. Wal-Mart says its ultimate goal is to reduce packaging by 5 percent over 2006 levels by 2013.

Yet another new green project being implemented by Wal-Mart involves offering customers more green product choices. Not only has this resulted in Wal-Mart stores offering low-priced organic foods, but Wal-Mart has now become the world's biggest purchaser of organic cotton. The company's stores are also offering a large variety of energy-efficient light-bulbs, which are displayed prominently with information that helps consumers calculate how much money they can save by simply changing the bulbs in their homes. Additionally, Wal-Mart has announced that it will begin using a "sustainability index" to measure the environmental impact of the products it sells in its stores. Using this information, customers will be able to choose products that are more environmentally friendly.

Many environmentalists, however, are skeptical of Wal-Mart's recent green conversion. For years, the company has been viewed by activists as a plunderer of the environment whose rapid growth used up natural resources, contributed to urban sprawl, sucked up electricity, and contributed to global warming. The company has come under the most heated attack from environmentalists for buying too many of its products from distant places such as China, products that require long-distance shipping, which adds to the world's carbon emissions. China's government also is very lax when it comes to the impact of its manufacturing industries on air and water quality. Other widely publicized criticisms of Wal-Mart include its low pay and mistreatment of workers.

And even with recent green changes, some in the environmental movement point out that the company continues to have a dramatic negative impact on the environment. Each day, many of Wal-Mart's thousands of stores are still open twenty-four hours; hundreds of trucks carry shipments to and from its 118 distribution centers; and products continue to be purchased from around the globe. In addition, it is difficult to measure exactly what the environmental impact is for many of the company's touted green products. Environmentalists worry that Wal-Mart's green efforts may be only window dressing designed to impress consumers rather than a sincere transition to sustainability.

Certainly Wal-Mart, like other retailers, can expect to reap public relations benefits from its efforts to create a green image. In fact, because of recent criticisms, Wal-Mart may have even more reason to improve its image with green marketing, therefore, an argument can be made that the company's green programs may be just a passing ad campaign. On the other hand, many of the energy-saving changes and other initiatives being made by Wal-Mart do have a measurable environmental impact, and at the same time, can save the company money. Less packaging, for example, translates into lower shipping costs and less waste, reducing expenses. And if a retailer the size of Wal-Mart—a chain that operates across the nation and around the world—can make permanent, significant changes in the way it does business, the environmental impact could be dramatic.

Throughout its history, Wal-Mart has been known as an aggressive negotiator with suppliers and a powerful player in the business marketplace. If the company puts this power to work for the good of the planet, market watchers admit that the results could change the face of American business. Already, some observers see ripple effects in other companies. For example, Procter & Gamble is working to reduce its packaging on products such as Tide laundry detergent, and Hewlett-Packard, which sells computers and other high-tech equipment to Wal-Mart, has consulted with Wal-Mart on its packaging strategy.

Wal-Mart's green initiatives are representative of the ways in which the green movement is affecting a number of industries and their customers. The authors of the viewpoints in this chapter address this critical issue of whether and how the green movement might benefit the economy.

The Green Business Movement Is Taking Off

Michael S. Rosenwald

Journalist Michael S. Rosenwald writes for the Washington Post.

Keith Ware dressed naturally to set up his booth at the Green Festival. He wore an organic cotton hooded jacket, organic cotton blue jeans and organic hemp work boots, the soles of which are made from recycled surgical gloves. He was not, however, wearing his organic cotton underwear.

"That's not to say I don't own some," he said.

Ware is one of the owners of Eco-Green Living, a [Washington, D.C.] Logan Circle store that sells organic and fair-trade products such as teas, hemp boots and even the makeshift floor he was setting up, which was made from Marmoleum—a combination of linseed oil, wood flour, rosin, jute and limestone. He was an exhibitor over the weekend at the Green Festival, which drew crowds of people to the Washington Convention Center to celebrate lightbulbs that last 60,000 hours, investment funds targeting socially responsible companies and paper made from elephant dung by a company called Mr. Ellie Pooh.

By many accounts, the green business movement is taking off, with the marketplace topping more than $228 billion in the United States.

The show, the third in the District [of Columbia], grew from 250 exhibitors in the first year to more than 350. Although some exhibitors were selling products, the chief inten-

Michael S. Rosenwald, "Showcasing the Growth of the GreenEconomy," *The Washington Post*, October 16, 2006, p. D01. Copyright © 2006, The Washington Post. Reprinted with permission.

tion of the show was to develop the industry by connecting the principles and products of green businesses with mainstream customers.

The Growing Green Economy

By many accounts, the green business movement is taking off, with the marketplace topping more than $228 billion in the United States and with such companies as Wal-Mart getting into organic food and General Electric Co. [GE] plowing into renewable energy. Levi's is introducing organic cotton jeans. *Vanity Fair* recently published a green issue.

"I think the business has taken off like a rocket," said Kevin Danaher, cofounder of Global Exchange, a San Francisco organization that promotes social, economic and environmental justice around the world. "I think it's left the launching pad."

What was long a counterculture [green] movement is now embracing one of its sworn enemies—big business—as a key component of the cause.

But as Danaher and others pound away at expanding the green economy, what was long a counterculture movement is now embracing one of its sworn enemies—big business—as a key component of the cause. Danaher's organization has railed for years against Nike Inc.'s manufacturing methods, accusing the company of running sweatshops, yet he says the Wal-Marts of the world can help the world go green. Such companies legitimize the movement and can offer a wider market for niche products from smaller companies, he said.

"It's the big guys genuflecting in the reflection of our values," he said. "The previous economy was based on money values. The next economy will be based on life values. You do commerce and make money, but you're making your money by saving nature and protecting human rights."

Danaher acknowledged that embracing big business may seem contradictory, and not all green groups agree with him. Wal-Mart has plenty of critics, who argue that the retailer's drive for low-cost products could degrade organic standards. "It creates confusion," Danaher said. "People have this anti-corporation, anti-big thing, which is understandable. Wal-Mart knocks out small businesses. They keep their wages down." But, he said: "They get it out into the public mind. That's why we do this show. Let's get into the general public. Preaching to the already converted doesn't take you anywhere. It's taking it into the mainstream that does."

Wal-Mart ... has invested heavily in its organic business, becoming the world's largest buyer of organic cotton products.

Ware's store has been open for about a year. Besides selling to walk-in customers, the store supplies home building and remodeling contractors with tankless water heaters, solar-powered roof fans, bamboo flooring and nontoxic paints. "We have grown phenomenally," he said. "We've gone from doing a couple hundred dollars a month to several thousand a day."

Competition from Big Business

One of the most common questions Ware gets about his business is about competition, particularly from big companies. Wal-Mart, for example, has invested heavily in its organic business, becoming the world's largest buyer of organic cotton products. Last year [2005], GE said that its Ecomagination program, which it describes as building "innovative technologies that help customers address their environmental and financial needs and help GE grow," generated $10.1 billion in revenue, up from $6.2 billion in 2004. Waste Management Inc., the country's largest waste collector, is turning landfill gases into electricity for 400,000 homes.

"People always ask me about competition," Ware said. "No. No. There is only validation of the industry right now. It hurts the movement if they are doing small things for the publicity. If they are genuinely trying to do the things that they say they are doing for the right reasons, then it helps. I'm sure they are finding that, heck, they are earning more money off it. The idea is to get everybody moving."

Which raises the question: What if Target or Wal-Mart opened a store 10 blocks from him that sold everything he sells?

Ware doesn't think Wal-Mart would put him out of business. In fact, he thinks if Wal-Mart sells more green products, his business will be enhanced, with even more foot traffic. Ware said that if competitors were legitimately green, "I would be absolutely enthralled with it. . . . I know there will be more and more places coming up where you can buy Marmoleum flooring. Everyone will soon be selling organic cotton shoes and clothing."

A Diverse Market

And judging by the turnout at this year's show, there will be plenty of customers. The festival drew about 25,000 people, up from 17,000 last year. Fifteen minutes after opening Saturday morning, there were four lines with more than 60 people in each, waiting to get tickets.

The green industry's move toward the middle provided an interesting study in contrasts. While the show offered free valet parking for bicycle riders, high-profile Washington was also represented, and [prominent television journalist] Tim Russert and his wife strolled through the hall.

Liz and Jim Staedler of Summit, New Jersey, were in town visiting their daughter when they came across a flier for the show. Though they have never been to a green event, their 22-

year-old son has been pushing them to incorporate sustainable energy into their . . . home. They decided to drop by for some ideas.

"I thought it would be hippies and granolas, that type of thing," Jim said. "What I see here is some of that, but it's really more toward the mainstream."

The Staedlers were standing in an aisle with a booth selling politically charged bumper stickers, including one that said "Too Poor To Vote Republican." But nearby, in a booth with an iPod playing the Jackson Five through a speaker, a tall man in a pinstriped suit introduced chic body products from Pangea Organics. Big selling point: The skin lotion boxes are plantable and will grow Genovese sweet basil.

The products displayed varied appreciably: stationery from Mr. Ellie Pooh; organic wine and beer; sustainable men's underwear at $10 a pair. There was wheat litter bedding for pets, organic yerba mate, and information on obtaining an MBA [master of business administration] in sustainable management.

Zach Lyman is the managing partner of a District [of Columbia] company called Reware, which sells backpacks and messenger bags that have small solar panels on the outside to provide electricity for charging. Connect cell phones, iPods, GPS [global positioning system] navigation devices and other gizmos to the bag, and they can be charged in generally the same time it would take plugging them into a wall socket. The bags sell for about $240. Lyman estimated that he has sold about 3,500 of them.

The bags were popular with early adopters and green-product aficionados, but after Hurricane Katrina, when millions of Americans realized that they could be without power for months, Lyman's business expanded into the mainstream, to average consumers as well as disaster workers and utility companies.

"I'm a big mainstream guy," Lyman said. "That's the whole thing with this bag. How do we introduce renewable energy to people who don't think about it in their everyday life?"

Lyman said he was particularly enthusiastic, about GE's efforts in green energy.

"My whole goal in life is to bring this stuff into the mainstream," he said. "I look at GE and I'm excited. They are getting the message out, and for us, here you have one of the most successful companies in the world and they are saying that climate change matters, that renewable energy matters. That is so exciting."

Mark Bisbee, the owner of Liberty Carpet One in Fairfax [Virginia], has created an offshoot called GreenFloors. He sells, among other things, carpet made from recycled soda bottles, which are sorted by color, ground into chips that are turned into fibers, then spun into a carpet.

A curious thing happened in the carpet market. Because nylon carpet needs oil for production, the high price of oil has pushed nylon carpet prices about $3 per square yard above recycled carpet.

Bisbee has customers in 48 states. He is still waiting for Wyoming and Hawaii.

"It was a small niche market and now it's more mainstream," Bisbee said. "Basically it's a question of awareness. Once people are aware they have choices it's easy, especially if it's economically similar. Then there is not really a decision."

A Green Economy Will Produce Many New Green Jobs

John Podesta

John Podesta is president and chief executive officer of the Center for American Progress, a progressive think tank.

The signs are clear: Our economy is in trouble. Falling home prices, foreclosures, bank failures, a weaker dollar, rising prices for gas, food, and steel, and layoffs in banking, construction, and manufacturing sectors are all indicators of serious economic strain—following a long period in which the middle class went nowhere even while the economy grew as a whole. What's more, evidence suggests the current downturn will continue for at least another year.

At the same time, we face a growing climate crisis that will require us to rapidly invest in new energy infrastructure, cleaner sources of power, and more efficient use of electricity and fuels in order to cut global warming pollution. There is much work to be done in building smart solutions at a scale and speed that is bold enough to meet this gathering challenge.

We face a growing climate crisis that will require us to rapidly invest in new energy infrastructure, cleaner sources of power, and more efficient use of electricity and fuels.

It is time for a new vision for the economic revitalization of the nation and a restoration of American leadership in the

John Podesta, "Green Recovery: A New Program to Create Good Jobs and Start Building a Low-Carbon Economy," Center for American Progress, September 9, 2008. This material was created by the Center for American Progress. www.americanprogress.org.

world. We must seize this precious opportunity to mobilize the country and the international community toward a brighter, more prosperous future. At the heart of this opportunity is clean energy, remaking the vast energy systems that power the nation and the world. We must fundamentally change the way we produce and consume energy and dramatically reduce our dependence on oil. The economic opportunities provided by such a transformation are vast, not to mention the national security benefits of reducing oil dependence and the pressing need to fight global warming. The time for action is now.

A new green recovery program that spends $100 billion over two years would create 2 million new jobs, with a significant proportion in the struggling construction and manufacturing sectors.

Today, the Center for American Progress [CAP] releases a new report by Dr. Robert Pollin and University of Massachusetts [Amherst] Political Economy Research Institute economists. This report demonstrates how a new green recovery program that spends $100 billion over two years would create 2 million new jobs, with a significant proportion in the struggling construction and manufacturing sectors. It is clear from this research that a strategy to invest in the greening of our economy will create more jobs, and better jobs, compared to continuing to pursue a path of inaction marked by rising dependence on energy imports alongside billowing pollution.

The $100 billion fiscal expansion that we examined in this study provides the infrastructure to jump-start a comprehensive clean energy transformation for our nation, such as the strategy described in CAP's 2007 report, *Capturing the Energy Opportunity: Creating a Low-Carbon Economy*. This paper shows the impact of a swift initial investment in climate solutions that would direct funding toward six energy efficiency and renewable energy strategies:

- Retrofitting buildings to increase energy efficiency

- Expanding mass transit and freight rail

- Constructing "smart" electrical grid transmission systems

- Wind power

- Solar power

- Advanced biofuels

This green recovery and infrastructure investment program would:

- Create 2 million new jobs nationwide over two years.

- Create nearly four times more jobs than spending the same amount of money within the oil industry and 300,000 more jobs than a similar amount of spending directed toward household consumption.

- Create roughly triple the number of good jobs—paying at least $16 dollars an hour—as spending the same amount of money within the oil industry.

- Reduce the unemployment rate to 4.4 percent from 5.7 percent (calculated within the framework of U.S. labor market conditions in July 2008).

- Bolster employment especially in construction and manufacturing. Construction employment has fallen from 8 million to 7.2 million over the past two years due to the housing bubble collapse. The green recovery program can, at the least, bring back these lost 800,000 construction jobs.

- Provide opportunities to rebuild career ladders through training and workforce development that if properly implemented can provide pathways out of poverty to those who need jobs most. (Because green investment not only creates more good jobs with higher wages, but more jobs overall, distributed broadly across the economy, this program can bring more people into good jobs over time.)

- Help lower oil prices. Moderating domestic energy demand will have greater price effects than modest new domestic supply increases.

- Begin the reconstruction of local communities and public infrastructure all across America, setting us on a course for a long-term transition to a low-carbon economy that increases our energy independence and helps fight global warming. Currently about 22 percent of total household expenditures go to imports. With a green infrastructure investment program, only about 9 percent of purchases flow to imports since so much of the investment is rooted in communities and the built environment, keeping more of the resources within the domestic economy.

Our report looked at investments that were funded through an increase in near-term government spending, which could ultimately be repaid by future carbon cap-and-trade revenues. These sources of new investment included the following funding mechanisms:

- *$50 billion for tax credits.* This would assist private businesses and homeowners to finance both commercial and residential building retrofits, as well as investments in renewable energy systems.

- *$46 billion in direct government spending.* This would support public building retrofits, the expansion of mass transit, freight rail, smart electrical grid systems, and new investments in renewable energy.

- *$4 billion for federal loan guarantees.* This would underwrite private credit that would be extended to finance building retrofits and investments in renewable energy.

A comprehensive clean energy agenda is essential to the future of our country. The green recovery and infrastructure investment described here is doable in the early days of a new administration. It would enable our country to take significant steps, through energy efficiency and renewable energy development, to move toward a low-carbon economy, while Congress and the next administration move toward the swiftest possible implementation of an economy-wide greenhouse gas cap-and-trade program.

A comprehensive clean energy agenda is essential to the future of our country.

The next president and lawmakers can pledge to repay the Treasury the cost of the green infrastructure recovery program from cap-and-trade auction revenue. The plan increases public spending in the short term when a near-recession economy needs greater impetus to growth; but it remains consistent with a fiscally responsible long-term plan to reduce the debt as a share of GDP after the economy recovers.

My colleagues and I at CAP look forward to continuing to work on our shared mission to reap all of the benefits provided by the transition to a low-carbon economy and look forward to discussing this work in greater detail.

A Green Economy Could Lift Millions Out of Poverty

Preeti Mangala Shekar and Tram Nguyen

Preeti Mangala Shekar is a communications associate at the Global Fund for Women, a grant-making foundation that supports women's rights organizations. Tram Nguyen is the executive editor of ColorLines, *an online magazine on race and politics.*

Climate change is the 21st century's wake-up call to not just rethink but radically redo our economies. Ninety percent of scientists agree that we are headed toward a climate crisis, and that, indeed, it has already started. With the urgent need to reduce carbon emissions, the clean energy economy is poised to grow enormously. This sector includes anything that meets our energy needs without contributing to carbon emissions or that reduces carbon emissions; it encompasses building retrofitting, horticulture infrastructure (tree pruning and urban gardening), food security, biofuels and other renewable energy sources, and more.

Green Jobs for People of Color

It's becoming clear that investing in clean energy has the potential to create good jobs, many of them located in urban areas as state and city governments are increasingly adopting public policies designed to improve urban environmental quality in areas such as solar energy, waste reduction, materials reuse, public transit infrastructures, green building, energy and water efficiency, and alternative fuels.

According to recent research by Raquel Pinderhughes, a professor of urban studies at San Francisco State University, green jobs have an enormous potential to reverse the decades-long trend of unemployment rates that are higher for people of color than whites. In Berkeley, California, for example, unemployment of people of color is between 1.5 and 3.5 times that of white people, and the per capita income of people of color is once again between 40 to 70 percent of that of white people.

It's becoming clear that investing in clean energy has the potential to create good jobs, many of them located in urban areas.

Pinderhughes defines green-collar jobs as manual labor jobs in businesses whose goods and services directly improve environmental quality. These jobs are typically located in large and small for-profit businesses, nonprofit organizations, social enterprises, and public and private institutions. Most importantly, these jobs offer training, an entry level that usually requires only a high school diploma, and decent wages and benefits, as well as a potential career path in a growing industry.

Yet, though green economics present a great opportunity to lift millions of unemployed, underemployed or displaced workers—many of them people of color—out of poverty, the challenge lies in defining an equitable and workable development model that would actually secure good jobs for marginalized communities.

"Green economics needs to be eventually policy-driven. If not, the greening of towns and cities will definitely set in motion the wheels of gentrification," Pinderhughes adds. "Without a set of policies that explicitly ensures checks and measures to prevent gentrification, green economics cannot be a panacea for the ills of the current economy that actively displaces and marginalizes people of color, while requiring their cheap labor and participation as exploited consumers." . . .

A Fundamental Transformation Is Needed

What remains to be seen is how green economics will transition out of current prevalent models of ownership and control. A greener version of capitalism could possibly address some of the repercussions of a consumption economy and the enormous waste it generates. But critics and activists also worry that a "replacement mind-set" is largely driving the optimism and energy of greening our industries and jobs. Hybrid cars replace conventional cars, and organic ingredients are promised in a wide variety of products from hand creams to protein bars. Many mainstream environmental festivals like the popular Green Festival held in San Francisco, Washington, D.C., and Chicago, have yet to embrace a democratic diversity. Peddling wonderful green products and services that will reduce your ecological footprint, are accessible, alas, only to elite classes that are predominantly white.

Green jobs have an enormous potential to reverse the decades-long trend of unemployment rates that are higher for people of color than whites.

"An authentic green economics system is one that would mark the end of capitalism," notes B. Jesse Clarke, editor of *Race, Poverty and the Environment*. And one that would ensure labor rights and organizing, collective ownership and equality are all at the heart of it, he adds. "The real green movement has not started yet."

A movement toward economic justice requires the mobilizing and organizing of the poorest people for greater economic and political power. A good green economic model would surely be one where poor people's labor has considerable economic leverage. "Wal-Mart putting solar panels on its store roofs is not a solution," says Clarke. "We need real solutions and strong measures—carbon taxes on imports from China would considerably reduce the incentive of cheap imports and make a push to produce locally."

"Green economics can create a momentum—a political moment akin to the civil rights movement. But unless workers are organized, any success is likely to be marginal. So the key problem is in organizing a political base," adds Clarke.

Green economics, then, is not just a green version of current economic models, but a fundamental transformation, outlines Brian Milani, a Canadian academic and environmental expert who has written extensively on green economics. He writes in his book *Designing the Green Economy*: "Green economics is the economics of the real world—the world of work, human needs, the earth's materials, and how they mesh together most harmoniously. It is primarily about 'use value,' not 'exchange value' or money. It is about quality, not quantity, for the sake of it. It is about regeneration—of individuals, communities, and ecosystems—not about accumulation, of either money or material."

Peddling wonderful green products and services that will reduce your ecological footprint, are accessible, alas, only to elite classes that are predominantly white.

Carbon Caps Represent Real Change

The $125 million promised through the Green Jobs Act is admittedly a drop in the bucket as far as the amount of financing and infrastructure needed to implement green jobs, activists say. Among the Democratic presidential candidates [of 2008], all of whom have proposals for clean energy investment, talk has run into the billions of dollars for green economic stimulus.

So who will pay to get the green economy going and train a green workforce? Throughout history, we have freely released carbon and other greenhouse gasses into the atmosphere and not had to pay a penny for the privilege. Industrial polluters and utilities may face fines for toxic emissions or releasing hazardous waste, but there has been no cost for emitting carbon as a part of day-to-day business. However, we have come to find that the atmosphere is a limited resource, and it's getting used up fast.

A movement toward economic justice requires the mobilizing and organizing of the poorest people for greater economic and political power.

By limiting the total amount of carbon that can be released, and making industries pay for their pollution, global warming policies finally recognize that the atmosphere has value and must be protected. The policy with the most momentum in the United States and around the world is to "cap and trade" the amount of carbon that can be emitted every year. With this policy, the government sets a hard target for CO_2 [carbon dioxide] emissions, and then companies have to trade credits to get back the right to emit that carbon, no longer for free.

One often overlooked fact, though, is that under a cap-and-trade policy, a tremendous amount of money could change hands—the Congressional Budget Office estimates that the new value created by such a policy ranges from $50–$300 billion each year. So far, public debate has focused on setting targets and caps, but the question of who will benefit from those credits has largely been ignored. In fact, many proposals have simply given these valuable new property rights away to polluters for them to sell to each other, because they were the ones who were polluting to begin with.

Under an important variant of the cap-and-trade policy called "cap and auction," the government not only limits the total carbon emissions, but it also captures the value of those carbon credits for public purposes by requiring that all polluters must bid for and buy back the right to emit. A 100-percent auction of permits would give the public ready access to the ongoing funds we will need to reinvest in social equity and bring down poor people's energy bills, or to support new research, or to launch new projects that not only establish training for green jobs, but create those jobs themselves, rebuilding the infrastructure of our communities for a clean energy economy.

However, there can be a lot of slippage between the green economy and green jobs that actually go to workers of color, especially in today's anti–affirmative action context. In one pilot program, nearly two dozen young people of color were trained to install solar panels, but only one got a job. Ultimately, employers can't be told who to hire, though there are some ideas about providing incentives, like requiring companies to show they hire locally and diversely before public institutions will invest their assets there.

Developing Good Green Jobs

"Green for All," the campaign launched in September 2007 by the Ella Baker Center [for Human Rights] and other partners like Sustainable South Bronx and the Apollo Alliance, is currently among the leading advocates pushing for policy that would ensure a racially just framework for green economics to grow and flourish, without which, green economics can end up being just a greening consumption. With a goal to bring green-collar jobs to urban areas, this campaign positions itself as an effort to provide a viable policy framework for emerging grassroots, green economic models. The campaign's long-term goal is to secure $1 billion by 2012 to create "green pathways out of poverty" for 250,000 people by greatly expanding federal government and private sector commitments to green-collar jobs.

"A big chunk of the African American community is economically stranded," [green activist] Van Jones said in the *New York Times* last fall [2007] as the campaign began. "The blue-collar, stepping-stone, manufacturing jobs are leaving. And they're not being replaced by anything. So you have this whole generation of young blacks who are basically in economic free fall."

Green economics . . . is not just a green version of current economic models, but a fundamental transformation.

The challenge of making the green economy racially equitable means addressing the question of how to build an infrastructure that includes not just training programs but also the development of actual good jobs and the hiring policies that make them accessible. How can we guarantee that all these new green jobs will go to local residents? As one activist admitted, "There's just no good answer to this so far."

Many of the answers will have to come in the doing, and the details, as green industry continues to take shape. There are plenty of ideas about how to create equitable policies, as outlined in the report *Community Jobs in the Green Economy* by the Apollo Alliance and Urban Habitat. They include requiring employers who receive public subsidies to set aside a number of jobs for local residents and partner with workforce intermediaries to hire them. Some cities are already requiring developers to reserve 50 percent of their construction jobs for local businesses and residents. Cities can also attach wage standards to their deals with private companies that are pegged to a living wage. In Milwaukee, [Wisconsin,] after two freeway ramps were destroyed downtown, a coalition of community activists and unions won a community benefits agreement from the city to require that the new development include mass transit, green building and living wages for those jobs.

As we have learned in many progressive struggles, communities need to be mobilized and actively involved in generating inclusive policies and pushing policy makers to ensure that green economic development will be just and equitable. Bracken Hendricks, a senior fellow at the Center for American Progress and coauthor of *Apollo's Fire: Igniting America's Clean Energy Economy*, says the green economy movement is still in its early stages of building public support. "There is not yet an organized constituency representing the human face of what it means to face climate change. There is an urgent need for a human face, an equity constituency, to enter into the national debate on climate change."

The challenge of making the green economy racially equitable means . . . the development of actual good jobs and the hiring policies that make them accessible.

Omar Freilla, founder of Green Worker Cooperatives, an organization that actively promotes worker-owned and eco-friendly manufacturing jobs to the South Bronx, is convinced that democracy begins at the workplace where many of us as workers and employees spend most of our time. "The environmental justice movement has been about people taking control of their own communities," he says. "Those most impacted by a problem are also the ones leading the hunt for a solution."

The Green Movement Is About More than Economic Issues

Environmental racism is rooted in a dirty energy economy, a reckless linear model that terminates with the dumping of toxins and wastes in poor communities of color that have the least access to political power to change this linear path to destruction.

Defining and then refining green economics as a way to steer it toward bigger change is at the root of understanding the sociopolitical and economic possibilities of this moment. Van Jones calls for a historic approach, one that considers the world economy in stages of refinement:

> Green capitalism is not the final stage of human development, any more than gray capitalism was. There will be other models and other advances—but only if we survive as a species. But we have to recognize that we are at a particular stage of history, where the choices are not capitalism versus socialism, but green/eco-capitalism versus gray/suicide capitalism. The first industrial revolution hurt both people and the planet, very badly. Today, we do have a chance to create a second 'green' industrial revolution, one that will produce much better ecological outcomes. Our task is to ensure that this green revolution succeeds—and to ensure that the new model also generates much better social outcomes. I don't know what will replace eco-capitalism. But I do know that no one will be here to find out, if we don't first replace gray capitalism.

The people most affected by the injustices of the polluting economy are already helping to lead the way, and it's business at its most unusual.

The Benefits to Green Marketing Are More than Hype

Stuart Atkins, MBA

Stuart Atkins is the owner of Atkins Marketing Solutions, a firm that provides marketing services for start-up businesses and organizations. He also teaches marketing at Chapman University and California State University, Fullerton.

The green movement, no matter where you land on the causes for global warming, makes good sense from a purely efficiency and management of resources perspective. Even if your product or service is not a "green-filled" solution, there are ways you can move in that direction. In a good or bad economy, this is a segment with strong growth potential. The business development potential is attractive and just makes sense. . . .

Green Marketing Works

Everywhere you read, search, listen, and watch, green is king. Whether it's saving gas, electricity, paper, or the planet—going green can mean greener pastures and thumbs when it comes to our environment and your company's bottom line. Green is in. Green is good.

However, with the ever-present emphasis on "greenness" also comes the need for how to communicate the enviro message. Does environmental messaging sometimes sound more like a fad than reality? Does your product line include features and benefits that are just waiting to be communicated? Are you forcing green features into your products that may not exist? Don't be green just to be green. It's more important to

Stuart Atkins, "Is the Green Movement Substance or Hype?" *Gerson Lehrman Group News* post, June 15, 2009. Reproduced by permission of the author.

be accurate rather than faddish regarding what your product or service offers the environmentally conscientious customer.

It's more important to be accurate rather than faddish regarding what your product or service offers the environmentally conscientious customer.

Here are some steps to recycle your marketing message so "zero waste" doesn't mean zero understanding. By taking the right steps you can conserve your energy, the planet's energy and your company's marketing resources.

Enviro Features and Differentiators

Perhaps your product has green marketing features you never realized. Ask yourself, "Are there features in my products that save energy, natural resources, and time?" If so, are you translating those features into your marketing messaging such as your Web site, white papers, product packaging descriptions and brochures?

For example, one of my clients sells a greenhouse controller technology that saves his customers water and electricity. Both water and power are resources that everyone likes to save. In this client's marketing and sales sheets, we made sure that phrases such as "decrease water and power usage while increasing your profits," were part of their green marketing speak.

What about your product packaging? Sometimes it's as simple as changing the type of clear clamshell packaging that saves your cost of goods and shipping fees, thus increasing profits while still helping the environment. Since newer types of clamshell plastic (the clear, plastic cover on many retail products) are easier to recycle, then you can discover added benefits in something as simple as your packaging. Older PVC [polyvinyl chloride] plastic used in clamshell packing has been attributed to health risks and is not "recycle friendly." PVC is considered eco-unfriendly. The alternative to PVC is called PET (polyethylene terephthalate). PET is easy to recycle and can be sealed through RF or heat sealing. In short, PET is eco-friendly and flexible. PET plastic has a built-in marketing story and speaks to environmental concerns.

In addition, even the type of paper and the design of your packaging can turn an old packaging design into a lighter, stronger, revised design that brings your packaging cost closer to the zero-waste goal that many companies, like Wal-Mart, are seeking. Many channel distributors and large retailers are requiring vendor adherence to zero-waste packaging. PET plastic is part of that requirement. If you don't comply, you don't qualify as a vendor.

Honesty, as in business and life, is the best policy when it comes to green marketing.

Reducing Printing Cost

Handing a customer sales slicks and product guides is still an effective way to sell product. Business cards and brochures will never go away. Yet, how many of us after returning from a trade show end up trashing the pounds of brochures and paper collected? One solution: Use your Web site as the repository source for your product literature. The digital text needs no trash can and requires no tree, little electricity and no paper to read. Printing only occurs if the customer chooses to. Post your critical marketing and product pieces in PDF [portable document] format on your resources or product page. If the customers choose to, they simply download the file for a later read or print. PDF is easily saved in a protected or encrypted format. Numerous PDF conversion utilities exist so you can convert Word, Excel, and PowerPoint files into a PDF version. The finished file looks clean and can even be saved in standard, medium and higher resolution formats. In standard format, large presentations become smaller for an e-mail attachment. The quality and resolution is more than satisfactory for most prints or reads.

Green Marketing Ethics

Honesty, as in business and life, is the best policy when it comes to green marketing. If your product or service is not environmentally friendly, then be careful not to stretch your messaging beyond the ozone layer. State your product benefits in simple and clear terms. Show examples of how your customer and the community benefit. If you have case studies, then use them as testimonials for your eco-friendly product or service. If your product just does not fit into the green marketing category, perhaps there are other ways you are moving toward zero waste or saving natural resources. If your company remanufactures 600 horsepower motors for late-model muscle cars, well, you are out of green marketing luck. But hold on, perhaps your company also has an accessory line of products and you changed the type of packaging plastic you use on those products. Now that might be a green marketing story to tell.

Your product or service does not have to be a full-bred-hybrid-econo-friendly-ozone-decreasing product to tell a green marketing story. Just by changing, in small ways, how you do business and go to market can make a difference.

Rethink your raw materials, packaging, and process to see where you can both tell a story and save the planet— not to mention your wallet!

For example, Arrowhead Mountain Spring Water Company recently redesigned an "Eco-Shape™ Bottle," as they call it. It has smaller waste to the bottle design, thus saving 30% of the plastic used for the same bottle size. That's simple imagination. That's green marketing and makes a great story.

Look for the Green Story

You may not have a big, jolly green marketing giant of a story, but I'll bet there are some areas you can audit for efficiency and change. Look for your story. Tell it. And remember, every little bit helps when we change our products and our marketing to greener pastures. Green marketing audits? Perhaps your products are about as eco-unfriendly as you can get. That could be an opportunity for a "green marketing audit." Rethink your raw materials, packaging, and process to see where you can both tell a story and save the planet—not to mention your wallet!

I have to admit, just the process of writing this article changed some of my brain's gray cells to green cells. No, not my hair, since I don't have enough to even dye green! There really is a marketing story to be told here. If your product or service is already green—or heading in the direction—then great. Evaluate how you are currently telling that story. From a product management and product life cycle standpoint, the benefits of a green, eco-friendly approach are worth the effort. Not only can you offer a product that serves a need, you can also offer a product that protects our environment. There are greener pastures on the other side of the marketing hill.

There Are Many Barriers to a Green Economy

Paul Hannam

Paul Hannam is the cofounder of Bright Green Talent, a recruitment agency for environmental business professionals. He is also the chairman and co-owner of Greenest Host, a Web hosting and marketing business.

There is mounting evidence of a green jobs revolution that promises to transform the workplace across the nation. Media pundits, business leaders, activists, and politicians claim that the green economy will create millions of new jobs, lead us out of recession and, in the process, transform our economy into a 21st-century engine of prosperity.

On the other hand, there is also a great deal of rhetoric and hype about this phenomenon and we should stand back and analyze what is really happening. The truth is that a massive economic transition doesn't happen overnight. Training and hiring millions of people for green jobs demands time, financial investment, and an adjustment of expectations about the very look and feel of a 21st-century labor force that is fostering sustainable change.

Many Barriers to a Green Economy

I have worked in the executive search and recruitment sector for over 20 years and in the environmental sector for 10 years. So I am very excited by the growth in green jobs and, in 2007, my partners and I founded a search firm called Bright Green Talent, which places environmental leaders and professionals in green organizations worldwide. Our understanding of the hurdles we've yet to overcome in this field comes from the

Paul Hannam, "The Challenges Facing Green Job Growth," *GreenBiz.com*, September 21, 2008. Reproduced by permission.

daily conversations we have with environmental and socially conscious companies about their needs and challenges.

As specialist recruiters in San Francisco and London, every day we see and wrestle with the emerging realities of the green labor market. For example, we see how America's lack of investment in engineering talent has left it short-staffed of renewable energy modelers and LEED [Leadership in Energy and Environmental Design] certified HVAC [heating, ventilation, and air conditioning] professionals to fuel this green labor revolution.

Going green [is] ... often perceived as an added burden in a tough economic time.

Indeed, there are a number of barriers to the development of the green economy and its creation of new employment. When we are able to overcome these barriers we will make major progress in our search for solutions to our most pressing environmental problems.

The Impact of a Recession. Sean Martin, a principal at Blu Skye Consulting, a sustainability consulting firm in San Francisco, says that their clients are adapting quickly to the troubled economy: "The nature of the requests [we receive] are getting much more focused on cost savings. While that element has always been there, it seems to be louder as of late."

Going green can lead to greater organizational efficiency and long-term cost savings, though it's often perceived as an added burden in a tough economic time. Companies that are driven by green missions are especially challenged to prove their worth and excellence. Credibility and long-term relationships are essential to encourage green innovation and, in the process, demonstrate to skeptics that green business practices truly do deliver a measurable return on investment.

Talent shortages. The lack of qualified workers is impeding the growth of many green industries, and there's little sign of relief. Bright Green works with Silicon Valley solar companies that have received tens (if not hundreds) of millions of dollars in venture-capital funding, but, even so, can't find experienced businesspeople to put that money to good use. The capabilities and knowledge needed to be successful are so new that even seasoned executives, brought into companies, often need a crash course in the art of effective, green business practice.

The lack of qualified workers is impeding the growth of many green industries, and there's little sign of relief.

To make matters more difficult, organizations are applying 20th-century hiring expectations to 21st-century industries. As recruiters we consistently have to address the gap between the perceived skill set necessary to succeed in a position and the reality of the marketplace.

What It Takes to Be a Green Employee

People simply don't have a dozen years' experience in solar system design or cleantech venture capital. These industries didn't exist back then, and even having five years' experience often means you're an old hand. As a consequence, employers are turning to candidates who have a track record in the general business, even if they have neither environmental experience nor even values. Ultimately, these folks may negatively impact their corporate culture as they may not care about the planet, and will end up harming a firm's credibility in the marketplace. The very people who are needed to grow these businesses sometimes risk compromising the mission of their new employers.

The green jobs movement will need to invest millions in training programs—and at times take calculated risks—in order to bring on board green employees who can both do a good job and help keep a company's reputation clean and green. Activists and policy makers who have long lobbied to see legislation passed that supports these programs still have a lot more to do.

What's become obvious from a human capital point of view is that credibility is the key to attracting not only consumers, but employees. Indeed, on many levels, it's the main competitive differentiator for both the consumers and employees in choosing a brand or company.

Companies are now having to be more accountable and authentic to maintain their green reputation.

Greenwashing. Companies are now having to be more accountable and authentic to maintain their green reputation. Many are seeing the green opportunity as a short-term branding opportunity and face mounting consumer and competitive pressure. The recent influx of "green" products in all categories makes it difficult for consumers to sort out who's green and who's not. Prospective employees also want to be reassured by the organization's green credentials.

Many graduates, as well as experienced professionals and executives, are looking to join a new hybrid organization that combines the entrepreneurial energies of a business with the compassion and impact of a nonprofit. These green social enterprises should flourish and help to develop a distinctive, emerging green workforce. There seems to be a profound passion and commitment to doing things differently, and many employees are looking for more than just a paycheck or a career. They see themselves as change agents, promoting more sustainable business practices, and "green jobs" seems to represent an exciting new labor market. Whatever it is, it's a new system that's inherently different from our current labor force.

Greenwashing ultimately hurts both industry and the planet and incongruent businesses will likely suffer over the long haul. Genuine talent will either look elsewhere or leave once the initial allure fades.

Regulation Must Push the Green Movement to the Next Level

The Need for Government Regulation. Underpinning—and at times unlocking—these challenges is the need for increased government policies, subsidies, and laws. Without these it will be difficult for sectors like renewable energy to prosper.

Without [increased government policies, subsidies, and laws] . . . it will be difficult for sectors like renewable energy to prosper.

Currently, fossil fuels receive enormous subsidies and many solar, wind, and other technologies are still in their infancy and need local, state, and, above all, federal support to flourish.

A clear and tangible commitment from Washington will be critical to ensuring the long-term viability of the green economy. Thankfully, 2009 promises to see more progressive regulation with both candidates embracing a forward-looking domestic energy agenda. Internationally, agreeing on a successor to the Kyoto Protocol [an international environmental treaty that aims to stabilize greenhouse gas concentrations in the atmosphere] and creating an international authority for carbon trading and investment will be positive next steps toward an integrated, stable global economy that properly accounts for carbon and guards against damaging environmental practices.

Indeed, change is afoot, and it's keeping both our hopes alive and spirits high.

As for the talent shortages, MBA [master of business administration] students are integrating the need for the green business skills into their core course work, with many programs now offering a "green business" track in sustainability to prepare their students for multifaceted, 21st-century leadership roles. The Aspen Institute reported this year [2008] that the percentage of MBA programs requiring their students to take courses focused on business and society issues jumped from 34 percent in 2006 to 63 percent in 2007.

Having built a business on the belief that our economy is capable of becoming truly sustainable, we're optimists. Despite the challenges, we're driving toward a green economy more quickly than anticipated. Green companies that focus on creating meaning in the workplace while delivering excellent quality products and services will continue to find the bright, talented people to lead their green teams in pursuit of greater market share and a greener planet.

Green Jobs Will Be Too Expensive

George Will

George Will is a Washington, D.C., columnist and television commentator.

The Spanish professor is puzzled. Why, Gabriel Calzada wonders, is the U.S. president recommending that America emulate the Spanish model for creating "green jobs" in "alternative energy" even though Spain's unemployment rate is 18.1 percent—more than double the European Union average—partly because of spending on such jobs?

Calzada, 36, an economics professor at Universidad Rey Juan Carlos, has produced a report which, if true, is inconvenient for the [Barack] Obama administration's green agenda, and for some budget assumptions that are dependent upon it.

Calzada says Spain's torrential spending—no other nation has so aggressively supported production of electricity from renewable sources—on wind farms and other forms of alternative energy has indeed created jobs.

Some American importers, seeking to cash in on the U.S. government's promotion of wind power, might be participating in an economically unproductive project.

But Calzada's report concludes that they often are temporary and have received $752,000 to $800,000 each in subsidies—wind industry jobs cost even more, $1.4 million each. And each new job entails the loss of 2.2 other jobs that are either lost or not created in other industries because of the political allocation—suboptimum in terms of economic efficiency—of capital.

An Economically Unproductive Idea

The president's press secretary, Robert Gibbs, was asked about the report's contention that the political diversion of capital into green jobs has cost Spain jobs. The White House transcript contained this exchange:

> Gibbs: "It seems weird that we're importing wind turbine parts from Spain in order to build—to meet renewable energy demand here if that were even remotely the case."

> Questioner: "Is that a suggestion that his study is simply flat wrong?"

> Gibbs: "I haven't read the study, but I think, yes."

> Questioner: "Well, then. (Laughter.)"

Actually, what is weird is this idea: A sobering report about Spain's experience must be false because otherwise the behavior of some American importers, seeking to cash in on the U.S. government's promotion of wind power, might be participating in an economically unproductive project.

Politically driven investments are economically counterproductive.

It is true that Calzada has come to conclusions that he, as a libertarian, finds ideologically congenial. And his study was supported by a like-minded U.S. think tank (the Institute for Energy Research, for which this columnist has given a paid speech). Still, it is notable that, rather than try to refute his report, many Spanish critics have impugned his patriotism for faulting something for which Spain has been praised by Obama and others. . . .

What matters most, however, is not that reports such as Calzada's and the Republicans' [a report by Republican Sen. Kit Bond, which has similar conclusions to Calzada's report] are right in every particular. It is, however, hardly counterintuitive that politically driven investments are economically counterproductive. Indeed, environmentalists with the courage of their convictions should argue that the point of such investments is to subordinate market rationality to the higher agenda of planetary salvation.

Still, one can be agnostic about both reports while being dismayed by the frequency with which such findings are ignored simply because they question policies that are so invested with righteousness that methodical economic reasoning about their costs and benefits seems unimportant. When the president speaks of "new green energy economies" creating "countless well-paying jobs," perhaps they really are countless, meaning incapable of being counted.

The Top Green Companies Are Also Major Polluters

Ash Allen

Ash Allen is a writer who contributes articles to 24/7 Wall St., a financial news and opinion Web site.

"Greenwashing" is the act of misleading the public regarding the environmental practices of a company or the environmental benefits of a product, service, or business line. Due to the public's increased awareness of environmental issues, including global warming, deforestation, and the loss of endangered species, greenwashing has become a staple of corporations' marketing efforts. All of the companies in this article have made some effort to address these concerns. Some of them appear to be trying harder than others, and even a few of them have made legitimate efforts to become responsible corporate stewards of the environment. Evidenced by the support of environmental groups and corporate responsibility professionals, many of these companies' green initiatives have made a positive impact.

These firms often spend millions of dollars on advertising to support the way that their companies are perceived in the green world.

A majority of America's largest companies have become part of the "green" movement. Some have fleets of hybrid trucks. Others install solar panels on their large buildings to consume energy more cost effectively with less of an impact on the environment. Many give generously to environmental nonprofit organizations.

Ash Allen, "The 'Green' Hypocrisy: America's Corporate Environment Champions Pollute the World," *24/7 Wall Street*, April 2, 2009. Reproduced by permission.

The irony of the "green" movement of US companies is that many of the firms that spend the most money and public relations efforts trying to show the government, the public, and their shareholders that they are trying to improve the environment are also among the most prolific polluters in the country. Pollution does not mean that the companies are doing anything illegal. Instead, it simply refers to natural consequence of the companies' industrial efforts which result in contamination to the air, soil or water by the discharge of substances that are toxic to the environment.

24/7 Wall St., [a business Web site] has put together a list of the Top Ten Greenwashers in America. There may be some large companies that are greater polluters than these firms. There may be other corporations that do more to promote their pro-environment credentials. But those can be counted on two hands.

> *According to the Environmental Protection Agency's Toxics Release Inventory (TRI), for the electrical equipment industry, GE [General Electric Company] was the fifth largest producer of chemicals . . . in 2007.*

Every company on this list makes a substantial investment in creating a perception that they are friendlier to the environment than their peers are or that they are on the side of good or that saving the global ecosystem should be part of a corporation's broad public responsibility—its good citizenship. These firms often spend millions of dollars on advertising to support the way that their companies are perceived in the green world. But, hidden behind these efforts, each corporation on this list is a Herculean polluter. And, that fact points to a hypocrisy which is almost completely hidden from the public. . . .

General Electric Is a Leader in Greenwashing

According to the Environmental Protection Agency's [EPA's] Toxics Release Inventory (TRI), for the electrical equipment industry, GE [General Electric Company] was the fifth largest producer of chemicals with four facilities in the top 100 generating 332,336 pounds in waste in 2007. In the miscellaneous manufacturing industry, GE's GE Osmonics facility was the fourth highest producing facility of TRI production-related waste with 1,919,437 pounds. According to the University of Massachusetts [Amherst] Political Economy Research Institute (PERI), General Electric is the sixth most toxic company when considering the amount of population exposed to its pollution and its toxicity level from its plants.

According to the EPA, "from approximately 1947 to 1977, the General Electric Company (GE) discharged as much as 1.3 million pounds of polychlorinated biphenyls (PCBs) from its capacitor manufacturing plants" at two facilities on the Hudson River. The EPA says that "the primary health risk associated with the site is the accumulation of PCBs in the human body through eating contaminated fish." The EPA has found that the cancer risk from eating fish from the Upper Hudson exceeds the EPA standard by 700 times.

On December 4, 2001, the EPA issued a "record of decision" calling for the dredging of 2.65 million cubic yards from the upper section of the Hudson River to remove approximately 150,000 pounds of PCBs. According to the company's Web site, "from 1990 to 2007 GE has spent over $1 billion in addressing PCB-related issues, with the majority of those expenses (82%) coming from just three sites," including the Hudson River. However, Riverkeeper and other not-for-profit organizations focused on the environment contend that GE has stymied the government's efforts to clean up the river and enforce the dredging requirement. In 2008, Alex Matthiessen, president of Riverkeeper, stated that CEO [chief executive officer] Jeffrey Immelt "continues to be, as is GE, very defensive about the Hudson River cleanup."

Each year the League of Conservation Voters [LCV] publishes the "Dirty Dozen," a program targeting candidates for Congress "who consistently vote against clean energy and conservation." Out of this list, GE's PAC [Political Action Committee] has donated thousands of dollars to six of the Dirty Dozen. Additionally, GE's PAC donated to two leading deniers of global warming, Senator Jim Inhofe, included in the Dirty Dozen list, and Congressman Joe Barton. . . .

American Electric Power Does Not Fulfill Its Green Promises

According to the company, American Electric Power's [AEP's] 2008 Sustainability Report is a "comprehensive report offering a frank discussion" about its environmental performance and its strategies for sustainability. . . .

As the report sets forth, "AEP's court-approved settlement of the New Source Review (NSR) litigation provides us with additional opportunities to reduce our power plant emissions." The complaint by the U.S. EPA and others alleged that AEP had made major modifications at some of its coal-fueled generating units without obtaining the necessary permits and without installing controls required by the Clean Air Act to reduce emissions of sulfur dioxide ("SO_2"), nitrogen oxide ("NOx"), and particulate matter. Despite the company's eagerness to be a leader in environmental conservation, "AEP did not admit to wrongdoing by agreeing to this settlement."

According to Frank O'Donnell, president of Clean Air Watch, an environmental policy group and whistleblower, "AEP is one of the nation's biggest polluters, now that GM [General Motors] is making fewer cars, and is one of the key lobbyist against political interest on global warming." O'Donnell also says that the company "aggressively seeks to block legislation unless it receives a huge financial windfall in the deal." The company's corporate PAC donated to five members of the Dirty Dozen as well as Congressman Barton. . . .

ExxonMobil Supports Groups That Deny Climate Change

Last week [March 2009], marked the 20th anniversary of the *Exxon Valdez* oil spill, the country's largest oil spill. As a result of the disaster, the ship spilled approximately 10.8 million gallons of crude oil into Prince William Sound, Alaska. Since that time, ExxonMobil has spent millions of dollars in an attempt to regain the public's trust. In an effort to continue to improve the way the company is perceived, it has begun to aggressively market its green initiatives. . . .

> *ExxonMobil has finally admitted that its funding efforts to research groups that deny global warming has an adverse effect on the environment.*

For some time, policy and research groups have worked to discredit the reality of global warming. According to the UK's [United Kingdom's] Royal Society, a highly regarded scientific academy, these groups "misrepresent the science of climate change by outright denial of the evidence." In 2007, the *Guardian* reported that academics were offered $10,000 each "by a lobby group funded by one of the world's largest oil companies to undermine a major climate change report due to be published today." Research performed by ExxonMobil watchdog, Exxpose Exxon, suggests that "since at least 1998, ExxonMobil has spent $17 to $23 million to bankroll these groups."

According to the company's *2008 Corporate Citizenship Report*, ExxonMobil has finally admitted that its funding efforts to research groups that deny global warming has an adverse effect on the environment. "In 2008 we will discontinue contributions to several public policy interest groups whose position on climate change could divert attention from the important discussion on how the world will secure the energy required for economic growth in an environmentally responsible manner."

On December 17, 2008, ExxonMobil settled an action with the EPA arising from Clean Air Act violations. As a result of the company's failure to monitor sulfur content in some fuel gas streams between 2005 and 2007, EPA tests found sulfur levels in excess of regulatory limits. This was a violation of a 2005 agreement. The total fine for the two EPA actions was more than $20 million. . . .

DuPont Products Put Human Health at Risk

On December 12, 2005, the EPA reached a $16.5 million settlement with DuPont arising from violations alleged by the agency that the company failed to report the possible health risks associated with perfluorooctanoic acid (PFOA), a chemical compound used to make Teflon. The settlement included $10.25 million civil administrative penalty and $6.26 million for Supplemental Environmental Projects [SEP]. According to the EPA, "A SEP is an environmentally beneficial project that the violator agrees to undertake in exchange for mitigation of the penalty to be paid." At that time, the penalty was the largest in the agency's history.

The violations alleged by the EPA included "multiple failures to report information to EPA about substantial risk of injury to human health or the environment that DuPont obtained about PFOA from as early as 1981 and as recently as 2004." The violations fell into three categories: human health information, environmental contamination, and animal toxicity studies. The enforcement action arose from DuPont's failure to disclose information that the company had obtained regarding the level of PFOA in 12 individuals who had been exposed to drinking water which contained the chemical. . . .

Archer Daniels Midland's Biofuels Do More Harm than Good

Biofuel, ethanol and biodiesel have quickly become the darlings of the green economy. They are heralded as renewable energy sources that some say can either reduce or entirely replace reliance on petroleum to fuel internal combustion engines. According to the company's [Archer Daniels Midland's (ADM's)] site, "a world in need of clean, renewable fuels to meet growing energy demand and achieve greater energy security is turning to agriculture for answers." As one of the largest diversified agribusinesses in the world, the company maintains that it has the necessary scale and expertise to be a leader in the production of biofuels. Its mission is "to unlock the potential of nature to improve the quality of life." ...

ADM publicly touts biofuels' green benefits, while failing to mention that the energy necessary to grow the corn requires significant amounts of fossil fuels, offsetting the environmental benefits.

The truth is that both ethanol and biodiesel emit less global warming pollution than burning petroleum-based gasoline. Unfortunately, producing biofuels creates enormous amounts of global warming pollution, so much so that many argue that they offset the benefits gained when the fuel is used to power engines. This is the sin of the hidden trade-off. In this case, a company promotes the green attribute of a product without consideration for other environmental factors. ADM publicly touts biofuels' green benefits while failing to mention that the energy necessary to grow the corn requires significant amounts of fossil fuels, offsetting the environmental benefits. According to the journal *Science*, "corn-based ethanol, instead of producing a 20% savings, nearly doubles greenhouse emissions over 30 years and increases greenhouse gases for 167 years. Biofuels from switchgrass, if grown on US corn lands, increase emissions by 50%." . . .

Waste Management Inc. Greenwashes Its Advertisements

According to Elizabeth Royte, a journalist for the Natural Resources Defense Council's *OnEarth*, since 2005, Waste Management Inc. has spent more than $90 million on TV commercials and print advertisements emphasizing the number of trees it saves through recycling, the amount of land it has set aside for wildlife habitats, and how much energy it generates through incineration. However, what the ads fail to disclose is that burning trash doesn't come without a price. Although the technology continues to improve, incinerators still discharge small levels of mercury, lead, and dioxin into the atmosphere. Royte also writes, "They also generate more carbon dioxide per megawatt-hour of energy generated than do power plants, and their ash is toxic." An additional consequence of incineration is that it discourages using landfills. Because power plants that use incinerators require a consistent flow of garbage, they are necessarily antagonistic to principles such as recycling, composting and reducing waste.

What [Waste Management Inc.'s] ads fail to disclose is that . . . incinerators still discharge small levels of mercury, lead, and dioxin into the atmosphere.

Waste Management's corporate PAC has donated to two members of the Dirty Dozen, [Senator] Mitch McConnell and [Congressman] Sam Graves. The company also made a donation to Congressman Barton. . . .

International Paper Continues to Expand Its Destructive Practices

According to TRI, for the paper industry, International Paper was the largest producer of chemicals with fifteen facilities in the top 100 generating 42,554,027 pounds in waste. The company also had the second highest producing facility of TRI production-related waste with 43,320,612 pounds. According to PERI, International Paper is the thirty-first most toxic company with a toxic score of 49,385.

According to TRI, for the paper industry, International Paper was the largest producer of chemicals with fifteen facilities in the top 100 generating 42,554,027 pounds in waste.

In 2008, the Rainforest Action Network [RAN] condemned a proposal by International Paper to build a pulp mill and establish 1.2 million acres of plantation forest in Indonesia's rain forest. This came as a surprise to RAN because the company had established an internal policy that it would not expand into Indonesia because it is a global warming and biodiversity hot spot.

Following the release, Thomas E. Gestrich, president of International Paper Asia, explained the company's plans in Indonesia. Mr. Gestrich said that he would prefer land that had already been cleared, but failed to explain how the company would secure hundreds of thousands of meters of forest without disturbing the natural habitat, waters or indigenous peoples.

Out of the LCV's Dirty Dozen, International Paper's PAC has donated thousands of dollars to five of the Dirty Dozen, including the leading denier of global warming, Senator Jim Inhofe. . . .

BP Does Not Act on Its Words

In December of 2000, CorpWatch, a nonprofit focused on corporate violations of environmental fraud, gave BP [formerly known as British Petroleum] a "greenwash" award. CorpWatch gives out the awards "to corporations that put more money, time and energy into slick PR [public relations] campaigns aimed at promoting their eco-friendly images than they do to actually protecting the environment." . . .

[Frank] O'Donnell has a poor opinion of the company's green initiatives saying "several years ago, BP, which probably spent as much as any company in the world to promote their green brand, was, at the same time, actively lobbying against efforts to limit global warming legislation—beyond petroleum and into the backrooms." In 2008, the company's corporate PAC contributed to half of the Dirty Dozen and to Congressman Joe Barton.

BP, which probably spent as much as any company in the world to promote their green brand, was, at the same time, actively lobbying against efforts to limit global warming legislation.

According to environmental watchdogs, things have not changed a great deal since 2000. A 2009 study published by Greenpeace reported that BP "allocated 93 percent ($20 billion) of its total investment fund for the development and extraction of oil, gas and other fossil fuels. In contrast, solar power was allocated just 1.39 percent, and wind a paltry 2.79 percent." Along with its aggregate investment in alternative energy—including wave, tidal, and biofuels—this amount is only 6.8 percent of BP's total investment. Greenpeace claims that this information is from internal company documents which it obtained.

As recently as last month [February 2009], BP entered into a settlement with the EPA stemming from charges related to violations of the Clean Air Act. According to Catherine R. McCabe, the acting assistant administrator for the EPA's Office of Enforcement and Compliance Assurance, "BP failed to fulfill its obligations under the law, putting air quality and public health at risk." She added, "Today's settlement will improve air quality for the people living in and around Texas City, many of whom come from minority and low income backgrounds." BP has agreed to invest at least $161 million on "pollution control, enhanced maintenance, and monitoring." Furthermore, the company must spend a total of $18 million, $12 million in civil penalties, and $6 million for supplemental environmental projects in the community. . . .

Dow Chemical Pollutes Public Spaces

In 2007, Dow [Chemical Co.] agreed to three EPA orders issued under the Superfund act [the Comprehensive Environmental Response, Compensation, and Liability Act (CERCLA)] for [dioxin] sediment cleanup on the Tittabawassee River [in Michigan]. However, despite this agreement, Dow Chemical has been slow to respond. As recently as 2008, the company claimed that it needed to measure the amount of the pollution before it could establish a cleanup program. Although the company removed contaminants from four environmental hot spots, particularly polluted areas, it has spent over $40 million on sediment sampling as well as other studies. According to the EPA, these areas include some of the highest dioxin levels recorded in the Great Lakes region. In July of 2008 an agreement was reached between Dow Chemical and the EPA to clean up dioxin contamination in the Riverside Boulevard neighborhood.

As of this year environmental groups and the EPA remain frustrated with the progress the company has made. In a March 3 EPA press release, the agency stated that "Dow Chemical Co. has agreed to conduct another Superfund removal action to clean up dioxin contamination in the Tri-Cities area." The project, focusing on the Saginaw Township's West Michigan Park, was scheduled to begin in mid-April and go through early June. According to a 2003 work plan issued to the Michigan Department of Environmental Quality [MDEQ], the park "is essentially a level field with an open expanse of grass for ball sports." The park includes picnic tables and a play area for children. According to the 2003 report issued by MDEQ on Dow's sampling study, the company found that the range of dioxin contamination in the soil in West Michigan Park was 140 to 670 ppt (parts per trillion) with an average of 413 ppt. In 2002, MDEQ established the residential action standard for soil containing dioxin at 90 ppt. According to the company's 2003 work plan, the planned interim measures included a hand-washing station and replacement of sand in children's play areas along with cosmetic measures.

In 2007, according to a study by the Union of Concerned Scientists, General Motors ranked as the second worst polluter, just above DaimlerChrysler, out of eight major car companies.

On March 2, Lisa P. Jackson, the new head of the EPA, sent a letter to community and environmental groups who had voiced concern over Dow's slow progress. She said that she would stop negotiations with Dow until EPA had been given the opportunity to take the groups' concerns into consideration. "My goal is to ensure an expeditious and robust cleanup, and I will take steps to ensure that the dioxin contamination is addressed in a manner that is protective of human health and the environment and that the process is open and transparent," she wrote. It has been a long time coming. . . .

General Motors Has Stood in the Way of Emissions Reduction

O'Donnell says "GM [General Motors] has long been one of the most anti-environment companies in America's history, dating back to its efforts to limit car emission standards. Because of their lobbying efforts, they created a loophole to reduce the average fuel economy of a carmaker's fleet." GM had legislation passed that provided "if you make a certain number of cars that are flex fuel—cars that can take both regular and biofuel—the average fuel economy of all of the company's cars can go down below emission standards. The loophole enables car companies to use ethanol as a pretext for reducing fuel economy." The company's corporate PAC donated to over seven of the Dirty Dozen and Congressman Barton.

In 2007, according to a study by the Union of Concerned Scientists, General Motors ranked as the second worst polluter, just above DaimlerChrysler, out of eight major car companies. In addition, GM manufactures the most cars that have 15 MPG [miles per gallon] or worse in city driving. In 2008 the numbers were not much better for GM. According to Greenercars.org, the American Council for an Energy-Efficient Economy's site for consumer research on the environment, GM's numbers have not improved. The company had the most car models on the list with four. Not surprisingly, the HUMMER H2, which is exempted from fuel economy regulations because it is considered heavy-duty, was rated number one.

Re-engineering the World's Energy System Will Be Difficult and Costly

Robert J. Samuelson

Robert J. Samuelson is a weekly columnist for the Washington Post, *an American newspaper.*

Few things are more appealing in politics than something for nothing. As Congress begins considering anti–global warming legislation, environmentalists hold out precisely that tantalizing prospect: We can conquer global warming at virtually no cost. Here's a typical claim, from the Environmental Defense Fund (EDF): "For about a dime a day [per person], we can solve climate change, invest in a clean energy future, and save billions in imported oil."

This sounds too good to be true, because it is. About four-fifths of the world's and America's energy comes from fossil fuels—oil, coal, natural gas—which are also the largest source of man-made carbon dioxide (CO_2), the main greenhouse gas. The goal is to eliminate fossil fuels or suppress their CO_2. The bill now [April 2009] being considered in the House would mandate a 42 percent decline in greenhouse emissions by 2030 from 2005 levels and an 83 percent drop by 2050.

A Difficult Undertaking

Re-engineering the world energy system seems an almost impossible undertaking. Just consider America's energy needs in 2030, as estimated by the Energy Information Administration (EIA). Compared with 2007, the United States is projected to have almost 25 percent more people (375 million), an economy about 70 percent larger ($20 trillion) and 27 percent more light-duty vehicles (294 million). Energy demand will be strong.

Re-engineering the world energy system seems an almost impossible undertaking.

But the EIA also assumes greater conservation and use of renewables. From 2007 to 2030, solar power grows 18 times, wind six times. New cars and light trucks get 50 percent better gas mileage. Lightbulbs and washing machines become more efficient. Higher energy prices discourage use; by 2030, oil is $130 a barrel in today's dollars. For all that, U.S. CO_2 emissions in 2030 are projected to be 6.2 billion metric tons, 4 percent higher than in 2007. As an example, solar and wind together would still supply only about 5 percent of electricity, because they must expand from a tiny base.

To comply with the House bill, CO_2 emissions would have to be about 3.5 billion tons. The claims of the Environmental Defense Fund and other environmentalists that this reduction can occur cheaply rely on economic simulations by "general equilibrium" models. An Environmental Protection Agency study put the cost as low as $98 per household a year, because high energy prices are partly offset by government rebates. With 2.5 people in the average household, that's roughly 11 cents a day per person.

The trouble is that these models embody wildly unrealistic assumptions: There are no business cycles; the economy is always at "full employment"; strong growth is assumed, based on past growth rates; the economy automatically accommodates major changes—if fossil fuel prices rise (as they would under anti–global warming laws), consumers quickly use less and new supplies of "clean energy" magically materialize.

There's no problem and costs are low, because the models say so. But the real world, of course, is different. Half the nation's electricity comes from coal. The costs of "carbon capture and sequestration"—storing CO_2 underground—are uncertain, and if the technology can't be commercialized, coal plants will continue to emit or might need to be replaced by nuclear plants. Will Americans support a doubling or tripling of nuclear power? Could technical and construction obstacles be overcome in a timely way? Paralysis might lead to power brownouts or blackouts, which would penalize economic growth.

Countless practical difficulties would arise in trying to wean the U.S. economy from today's fossil fuels. One estimate done by economists at the Massachusetts Institute of Technology found that meeting most transportation needs in 2050 with locally produced biofuels would require "500 million acres of U.S. land—more than the total of current U.S. cropland." America would have to become a net food importer.

Actually, no one involved in this debate really knows what the consequences or costs might be [of dealing with global warming].

Economic Make-Believe

In truth, models have a dismal record of predicting major economic upheavals or their consequences. They didn't anticipate the present economic crisis. They didn't predict the run-up in oil prices to almost $150 a barrel last year [2008]. In the 1970s, they didn't foresee runaway inflation. "General equilibrium" models can help evaluate different policy proposals by comparing them against a common baseline. But these models can't tell us how the economy will look in 10 or 20 years because so much is assumed or ignored—growth rates; financial and geopolitical crises; major bottlenecks; crippling inflation or unemployment.

The selling of the green economy involves much economic make-believe. Environmentalists not only maximize the dangers of global warming—from rising sea levels to advancing tropical diseases—they also minimize the costs of dealing with it. Actually, no one involved in this debate really knows what the consequences or costs might be. All are inferred from models of uncertain reliability. Great schemes of economic and social engineering are proposed on shaky foundations of knowledge. Candor and common sense are in scarce supply.

CHAPTER 3

Is Going Green Worth the Extra Costs to Consumers?

Chapter Preface

One of the key areas where technology could change the equation for green living is transportation—today one of the biggest contributors to global warming. Many consumers are eagerly waiting for the day when they can drive energy-efficient electric cars that do not require purchasing gasoline at often volatile prices and that do not release carbon pollution. That day suddenly seemed a little closer on August 11, 2009, when General Motors (GM) announced that its Chevrolet Volt electric car, due to debut in late 2010, will achieve a city fuel economy of 230 miles per gallon. The announcement has created a buzz in the car industry and among consumers, and it is likely to help GM recover from its recent bankruptcy and economic problems.

The Volt's rating of 230 miles per gallon is based on methodology developed by the Environmental Protection Agency (EPA) for rating plug-in electric cars. Under this new system, the EPA gives plug-in electric vehicles credit for traveling city miles mostly on electricity, evaluating this by kilowatt hours (kWh) per one hundred miles traveled. The EPA estimates that the Volt will consume as little as twenty-five kilowatt hours per one hundred miles in city driving, and at the average U.S. cost of electricity (approximately eleven cents per kWh), a typical Volt driver would pay about $2.75 for electricity to travel one hundred miles, or less than three cents per mile. Actual gas-free mileage, of course, might vary somewhat depending on the distances traveled and other factors, such as the weight in the vehicle and whether the air conditioner or other accessories are used.

The Volt's impressive fuel economy rating is due largely to the fact that it can travel up to forty miles on a full battery charge, using only electricity. The Volt basically has two modes of operation—electric and extended-range. In electric mode, the Volt is powered solely by a sixteen-kilowatt hour lithium-ion battery pack. When the battery charge is about halfway gone, the car automatically switches to extended-range mode, and a small gas engine kicks in to supply enough charge in the battery to power the electric motor. In other words, compared to a regular hybrid car that is powered by both electricity and a gasoline engine, the Volt is always running off the electric motor and the batteries. The leftover power in the batteries then can still be used to provide extra power during quick accelerations or on steep inclines. Including both electric and extended-range power, the car's overall range is estimated at around three hundred miles.

For many drivers, a vehicle like the Volt will allow them to drive on their daily commutes or errands using electric power only. The U.S. Department of Transportation has estimated that eight of ten Americans commute fewer than forty miles a day. The battery must be recharged periodically by plugging it into an ordinary electrical outlet—a process that GM says will take about eight hours. For the typical commuter, therefore, the car battery can be plugged in each night, giving it sufficient battery life to take them to their jobs and back the next day, gas-free—a scenario that seems almost too good to be true.

For longer trips, the Volt will still be very energy efficient, even with the use of the gas engine. Although official estimates of the fuel economy for highway driving and for combined city and highway use have not been completed for the Volt, GM executives have said that they expect the Volt will get more than one hundred miles a gallon in combined city and highway driving. No conventional gasoline-powered or hybrid car has ever been marketed that could get such a high mileage rating. Conventional gas-powered cars, for example, typically get only about twenty miles per gallon and even hybrids such as the Toyota Prius get only around forty-six miles per gallon.

The Volt has other advantages as well. People who have driven it say it has great acceleration and that it delivers full torque at all speeds. In addition, test drivers have said that the car handles extremely well, hugging the road and getting great traction. GM executives attribute this to the Volt's large, four hundred-pound battery pack, which is positioned under the back seats, giving the car a very low center of gravity and good weight distribution. And of course, because it is electric, the Volt is very quiet to drive since it runs on electricity from batteries. Best of all, when the Volt is in electric driving mode, it emits absolutely no carbon emissions that could contribute to climate change. Yet the car's true environmental value depends largely on how electricity is produced; if the electricity used to recharge the Volt's batteries comes from fossil fuels, there is still a negative impact on the environment, but if it comes from solar, wind, or some other renewable source, the environmental benefits are truly dramatic.

The major downside to the Volt, however, is the cost. GM estimates that pricing will start around $40,000, although government rebates of $7,500 may get the actual purchase price down to $32,500. At that price, critics say, it may not be cost effective for consumers to buy a Volt because even assuming gas prices go up to $4.00 per gallon, the overall cost per mile of driving would be much higher for a Volt than for a conventional, gas-powered car that has a much lower fuel economy. If the car is a hit with buyers, prices may come down in the future, but for now, the benefits of driving a Volt are primarily environmental, not financial. This question of whether green choices such as cars and other consumer goods are worth the extra costs to buyers is the subject of the viewpoints in this chapter.

Buying Green Products Pays Off in the Long Run

Yumi Araki

Yumi Araki is a writer who provides text for Bobvila.com, a home improvement Web site.

Purchasing pricier environmentally sustainable household items now might very well save the green on trees and in your wallet into the future.

According to the Organic Trade Association (OTA), a business and research group that represents organic industries such as propane torch manufacturer Flame Engineering and Bug Blocker Inc., which produces an environmentally safe pest repellent, organic product sales are slowing due to the economy but continue to increase overall as consumers become more knowledgeable about the environmental as well as economic benefits of sustainable purchases.

People are making the connection that buying environmentally sustainable purchases now, which are usually more expensive than their regular counterparts, will save money in the future.

Buy Now, Benefit Later

Barbara Haumann, OTA's press secretary, says that like other consumer markets "there's an economic downturn all around in the green industry," but that increasingly, "people are making the connection" that buying environmentally sustainable purchases now, which are usually more expensive than their regular counterparts, will save money in the future.

According to a recent report by Shelton Group, an advertising agency that conducts industry surveys of environmentally sustainable and energy-efficient initiatives, consumers are likely to take a number of energy-efficient measures after learning about how these products would save money over the long run. Upon discovering the benefits of higher-efficiency water heaters, for instance, 42 percent of consumers surveyed said that they'd be willing to install one in their homes.

A survey conducted by the Propane Education & Research Council (PERC) revealed that 57 percent of homeowners would be willing to invest in energy-efficient home appliances to lower monthly utility bills. It also showed that respondents were most interested in tankless water heaters, insulation technology and propane products.

In response to this increased interest, Energy Star [a program that sets standards for energy-efficient products] has worked with manufacturers to develop propane furnaces that use up to 15 percent less energy than standard models. According to the Environmental Protection Agency, Energy Star-labeled propane tankless water heaters with energy factors of 82 percent can save consumers up to 60 percent in energy bills.

"It's more expensive now [to purchase energy-efficient products], but the idea is that you get a better bang for your buck in the long run," says Henrik Selin, a Boston University international environmental politics professor.

Energy-Efficient Innovations

Green Home, an online resource of environmentally sustainable products and initiatives, reports that a standard 60-watt incandescent lightbulb's lifetime cost amounts to around $9 per megalumen-hour (a light energy and brightness measurement) and it costs $1. A 7.5-watt LED [light-emitting diode] lightbulb costs $100, but its lifetime cost amounts to around $4 per megalumen-hour.

Thomas Little, associate director of the National Science Foundation Smart Lighting Engineering Research Center at Boston University, is teaming with Rensselaer Polytechnic Institute and the University of New Mexico to investigate technologies that will accelerate the adoption of energy-efficient LED lighting, creating an environmentally viable substitute for incandescent lightbulbs. Little's team recently produced a prototype for wireless network signal-transmitting LED lightbulbs, which could significantly minimize light energy consumption while serving as a wireless hub for computers, smart phones and other devices. According to Ezdiyelectricity.com, LED lightbulbs cost 50 to 100 times more than incandescent ones but last almost 100 times longer.

Economic Obstacles

Despite the potential environmental benefits, Little says his team faces the challenge of making the innovation affordable.

> *[According to a recent survey,] 57 percent of homeowners would be willing to invest in energy-efficient home appliances to lower monthly utility bills.*

"When energy costs were high, people had a reason to turn to alternatives like taking the bus or riding your bike," Little says. Because energy prices have recently decreased, he explains, consumers have less incentive to invest in alternative energy resources compared to last summer [2008] when energy costs were very high. Little adds that funds have also diminished and one of his research sponsors is currently facing bankruptcy in the recent economic downturn.

"The economy is slowing access to money, but in spite of all that, there is interest and [companies] aren't giving up," he says.

Haumann remains hopeful that consumers will continue to show interest in green products and that consumer demand will spark producers to create more environmentally sustainable, energy-efficient products. At the end of 2008, the OTA reported an increase in consumer interest in organic cotton products, which typically range higher than regular cotton products in price but are manufactured with cotton that was cultivated using sustainable and non-pesticide farming techniques. "People have made the wider environment and health issue into a personal issue," says Haumann.

Bottom line: Purchasing slightly more expensive energy-efficient products now pays off in the long term.

The Extra Costs of Going Green on Consumer Products Are Often Justified

Kimberly Palmer

Kimberly Palmer is a senior editor and blogger for U.S. News & World Report, *a business and financial news magazine.*

Going green sometimes comes with a price: Organic vegetables can cost twice as much as their mainstream counterparts. So when is going green really worth it? We asked some top environmental experts to weigh in—and their answers might surprise you. They say that while spending extra is often justified, you can almost always find a cheaper alternative.

For home improvement projects, spending more can be better for the earth. Diane MacEachern, author of *Big Green Purse: Use Your Spending Power to Create a Cleaner, Greener World* and creator of the Web site Big Green Purse, paid about $1,500 extra for hardwood floors made of Brazilian cherry wood that had been approved for sustainability by the Forest Stewardship Council when she renovated her house a few years ago. She also paid about $600 extra for paint that was free of volatile organic compounds, or VOCs. But MacEachern says that choice actually saved her money because the lack of noxious chemicals meant that her family could stay in the house while it was being painted.

But there's also a cheaper option: MacEachern found carpeting made from recycled soda bottles, which looks and feels just like regular carpeting. "I looked at all these other options, and it turned out this was the easiest, cheapest, and quickest to install," says MacEachern.

"The greenest thing to do is as little as possible," says Maggie Wood, founder of the Jamesport, N.Y.-based Maggie Wood Design, a green home design consultancy. It's also usually the cheapest thing. For example, Wood explains, working with an existing house's footprint instead of knocking it down and starting from scratch is both more affordable and more environmentally friendly. She also recommends installing low-flow toilets and replacing lightbulbs with compact fluorescent lights, both choices that save money in the long term.

For home improvement projects, spending more [on green products] can be better for the earth.

When it comes to a big-ticket item such as kitchen cabinets, Wood often suggests that her clients look at purchasing "gently used" kitchen cabinets, which can be found through contractors or stores that sell salvaged pieces. Habitat for Humanity operates "ReStores" stocked with building materials that have been donated by contractors and other suppliers.

When it comes to organic food, the high price tag often provides health benefits. Recent research suggests that organic food is also more healthful food. The Organic Center, a nonprofit that collects research about organics, reports that according to recent studies, organic foods are more nutritious than their nonorganic counterparts 61 percent of the time. "Our position is moving in the direction of organic food being more nutritious," says Joe Dickson, the quality standards coordinator for Whole Foods. Although the company used to shy away from making that claim, Dickson says it is becoming more willing to do so because of the growing number of studies in the area.

But there's also a cheaper option: While organic food tends to be more expensive, MacEachern recommends looking for other items to trim from your budget, such as bottled water, in order to fit it into your budget. "It doesn't make any sense to say, 'I can't spend $3 more on organic milk, but I'm spending $20 a week on bottled water,'" she says.

Plus, since food sellers have to adhere to certain rules in order to label their products as organic, the organic food (and clothing) sold at discount stores such as Wal-Mart is just as green as the stuff sold at a higher-priced boutique.

When it comes to organic food, the high price tag often provides health benefits.

For personal hygiene and cleaning products, a higher price can mean fewer toxins. Jennifer Taggart, author of *Smart Mama's Green Guide,* suggests always checking out the ingredients of shampoo, body scrubs, and other products to avoid toxins, or shopping the organic aisle, where many of the products are made without those chemicals. But she says even products labeled "natural" can contain ingredients she tries to avoid, such as phthalates and parabens. The Web site www.cosmeticsdatabase.com allows users to look up certain products to check for their level of toxicity. Organic home cleaning products usually come without the powerful chemicals found in most mainstream cleaners, but they can also be more expensive.

But there's also a cheaper option: Make your own products. Taggart says there is no need to spend money on pricey products when you can make them yourself at home. In fact, Taggart makes her own perfume with essential oils because she avoids synthetic fragrances. She also creates body scrubs with sea salts and essential oils. Instead of buying air fresheners, she suggests cutting up an orange and simmering the peels on the stove. Pine needles or cloves work, as well. "You don't need to spend $6 on an air freshener," says Taggart.

For more intense cleaning around the house, Taggart suggests using baking soda and water mixtures or castile soap, which is made from vegetable oil, instead of store-bought products that usually run at least $5. "Don't be afraid to make your own homemade cleaners," she says. "It's how our grandmothers cleaned."

MacEachern has an even simpler solution: Use fewer products. "If you put everything that you use in one day on the counter, it will blow your mind," she says, adding that many people use as many as 25 products a day. Her advice? "Pick a day where you use none of that stuff—just brush your teeth and your hair, and forget about the rest."

There Are Few Extra Costs and Many Lasting Benefits to Green Building Design

Jennifer Crawford and Peter Morris

Jennifer Crawford is a research associate and Peter Morris is a principal consultant with Davis Langdon, a construction consultancy firm headquartered in London, England.

A recent study by the Pew Center on Global Climate Change estimates that the built environment is responsible for up to 40 percent of the United States' greenhouse gas emissions, which are a key contributor to global warming. While greenhouse gas emissions come from a variety of other sources, the fact that buildings are responsible for such a substantial amount indicates that if we want a healthier, more sustainable future, the way we plan and build buildings has to change. The primary source of building-related emissions is from the energy needed to build and operate them. While the most obvious energy usage comes from lighting, heating, and cooling the buildings during use, the extraction, manufacture, and transport of the materials required for construction also play a significant role. The construction of a building can contribute as much as 10 to 15 times the carbon emitted by the annual operation of that same building to the environment. In addition, construction waste, which is a significant percentage of waste in landfills, the amount of paving, and the associated loss of green spaces and natural habitat are also contributors to the negative impact buildings have on the environment.

Green Strategies Must Combat Climate Change on Many Levels

The transportation and urban infrastructure needed to maintain and operate facilities also contribute to [global warming]. The land area devoted to roads and parking in the United States is substantial, leading to a loss of habitat, heat trapping, and increased polluted runoff. Poorly planned urban growth has led to increased flooding as storm water runoff is increased and natural dissipation is decreased. And in urban areas with little green space but extensive paving, heat trapping can actually increase area temperature by several degrees.

The fact that buildings are responsible for such a substantial amount [of greenhouse gas emissions] indicates that . . . the way we plan and build buildings has to change.

In order to combat climate change, the United States must focus on cutting greenhouse gas emissions significantly and, to this end, a number of green strategies have been developed to assist companies and municipalities in reducing the greenhouse gas emissions associated with buildings, as well as reducing the impact of buildings on the overall environment. These include national systems such as LEED (Leadership in Energy and Environmental Design) and Green Globes, where buildings achieve levels (either through a voluntary rating system, such as with Green Globes, or a certification process, such as for LEED) by meeting certain design criteria, such as specified levels of water and energy efficiency, incorporation of renewable or recycled materials, etc.

Within these broader systems there are a number of more focused rating criteria established for particular building types (for example, LEED for Healthcare, LEED for Retail, LEED for Schools, and LEED for Homes), for improving existing building stock (such as LEED for Existing Buildings, which focuses on building operations, improvements, and maintenance; and LEED for Commercial Interiors, which focuses on tenant improvements), and for urban planning (such as LEED for Neighborhood Development).

While the complexity of these green strategies can vary widely, even small changes to the ways buildings are constructed and operated have been shown to have a noticeable effect, and more and more facilities planners and owners are proving that implementing green strategies can be both cost and environmentally effective.

Many project teams are building green buildings with little or no added cost and with budgets well within the cost range of non-green buildings with similar programs.

The Cost of Green Building

In 2007, [construction consultancy firm] Davis Langdon published *The Cost of Green Revisited,* which was an update to our earlier paper—*Costing Green: A Comprehensive Cost Database and Budgeting Methodology*—in which we examined the cost impact of incorporating sustainable design into building projects using the LEED rating system as the standard. In the first report, we compared the costs for over 100 laboratories, academic classroom buildings, and libraries—some that had actively attempted to achieve green and some that had not. After examining costs at a LEED point-by-point level, we concluded that there was no statistically significant difference in cost between buildings incorporating green features and those not. We also found that many project teams can build, and have already built, LEED-rated buildings within their existing budgets. This conclusion was reaffirmed in the updated report, which examined an additional 221 projects (this time expanding the pool of building types to include community centers and ambulatory care facilities along with academic buildings, laboratories, and libraries). The updated study shows essentially the same results as those found in the original 2004 study: There is no significant difference in average costs for green buildings as compared to non-green buildings.

Many project teams are building green buildings with little or no added cost and with budgets well within the cost range of non-green buildings with similar programs. We have also found that, in many areas of the country, the contracting community has embraced sustainable design, and no longer sees sustainable design requirements as additional burdens to be priced in their bids.

It is important to note, however, that in most of the buildings studied, the project teams tended to focus primarily on the lower or no-cost strategies—meaning the most expensive strategies were avoided. In addition, few buildings tended to strive for more than those levels of energy efficiency required by federal, state, or local ordinances. Despite the fact that construction costs overall have risen significantly over recent years, however, building owners are still actively finding ways to go green with little or minimal added cost.

[Green] buildings have many financial benefits . . . including reduced energy and operating costs, improved employee well-being, and reduced insurance costs.

Other studies have come to similar conclusions, that incorporating sustainable design features into projects adds little to no cost, and that many building owners build within budgets that do not include additional funds for sustainable features.

Financial Benefits Are Only the Beginning

The initial cost of a building is always important to any business wishing to expand their building space. As our report shows, green strategies can be incorporated into the building design, resulting in a cleaner, greener, healthier building at little or no initial cost. These buildings have many financial benefits that accrue over the life of the building, including reduced energy and operating costs, improved employee well-being, and reduced insurance costs. The long-term financial benefits combined with the low first cost can make green buildings contributors to the businesses' bottom line.

Green buildings can improve the financial status of some businesses in other ways as well. A recent study by CoStar found that LEED-rated buildings have a higher occupancy rate than non-LEED buildings, suggesting that more tenants prefer to rent space in green buildings than in non-green buildings. Interestingly, this study also reported that green buildings are able to garner higher rents than non-green buildings, suggesting that more tenants are willing to pay a premium for a cleaner, healthier space. Other studies suggest additional benefits, including improved happiness and well-being for the employee, and less sick time used.

As the realities of climate change have become more widely known and the impact of global warming on the health and well-being of people more of a concern, more and more cities and communities have been looking toward greener strategies to help minimize environmental impact and improve the quality of life for their citizens. The number of cities, counties, and regions instituting green strategies and requirements for buildings and infrastructure can only be expected to increase in the future.

These green strategies can have a huge impact on the economic competitiveness of cities and regions. Green buildings tend to be more energy and water efficient, and thus are more desirable by businesses and the public. Non-building green strategies, such as incorporating green spaces or improving or expanding public transit options, can help reduce traffic in congested areas, as well as improve air quality when fewer cars are on the road.

In addition, just as more businesses are showing a preference for green offices, more people are showing a preference for living in cleaner, greener cities and communities. As the cost of fuel continues to rise, public desire for more efficient buildings, better public transportation options, and better protection of green spaces, water, and other natural resources can be expected to also increase.

Incorporating green strategies into existing building space is . . . perhaps even more important than greening the new ones.

Greening Existing Buildings

While more and more new buildings are being built to meet environmentally friendly standards, new buildings still account for only a fraction of the total volume of the built environment within the United States. Incorporating green strategies into existing building space is, therefore, perhaps even more important than greening the new ones.

There are a number of LEED rating systems directed toward reusing existing buildings, including two previously mentioned, LEED for Existing Buildings and LEED for Commercial Interiors. But even buildings where owners are not prepared to attempt a LEED rating can still be made more environmentally friendly with minimal additional cost.

Strategies to green existing building stock can be as simple as swapping to more efficient lights and encouraging a reduction in waste as a company mandate or goal. They can also include more extensive strategies, such as retrofitting for more efficient heating and cooling systems. These can be very effective if done in conjunction with planned replacement or maintenance.

There are a number of additional strategies that companies can employ to become more green, which require no modifications to the buildings at all. These include providing incentives or assistance to employees to carpool or use public transportation; allowing flexible schedules and/or telecommuting; instituting recycling programs within their facilities along with an associated focus on reducing waste; requiring the use of nontoxic cleaning supplies; and transitioning landscaping to more drought-tolerant, native species.

The Green Imperative

While cost is always a consideration, the evidence is mounting that going green does not have to impact the financial bottom line. Thoughtful planning and design can make the transition to greener facilities easier, with a minimum of cost impact. In addition, even simple changes can lead to savings in energy used, carbon emitted, and money spent.

As the threat of global warming continues to grow, sustainable facilities and site planning are becoming more imperative. Embracing green design not only reduces the impact of buildings on the natural environment, but can also greatly benefit businesses in financial and nonfinancial ways.

Cap-and-Trade Legislation Will Create Only a Modest Increase in Homeowners' Energy Costs

Congressional Budget Office

The Congressional Budget Office is a legislative agency charged with reviewing congressional budgets and other legislative initiatives and providing advice to Congress about its budgetary implications.

Global climate change is one of the nation's most significant long-term policy challenges: Reducing emissions of greenhouse gases (GHGs) would moderate the damage associated with climate change and, especially, the risk of significant damage, but doing so would also impose costs on the economy. In the case of carbon dioxide (CO_2)—which accounts for 85 percent of U.S. GHG emissions—higher costs would stem from the fact that most economic activity is based on fossil fuels, which contain carbon and, when burned, release it in the form of that gas.

H.R. [House of Representatives bill] 2454, the American Clean Energy and Security Act of 2009, as reported by the House Committee on Energy and Commerce on May 21, 2009, would create a cap-and-trade program for GHG emissions, an incentive-based approach for regulating the quantity of emissions. (The bill would also make a number of other significant changes in climate and energy policy.) The legislation would set a limit (the cap) on total emissions over the 2012–2050 period and would require regulated entities to hold rights, or allowances, to emit greenhouse gases. After allowances were initially distributed, entities would be free to buy and sell them (the trade part of the program).

The Estimated Costs to Households from the Cap-and-Trade Provisions of H.R. 2454, Washington, DC: Congressional Budget Office, 2009.

This analysis examines the average cost per household that would result from implementing the GHG cap-and-trade program under H.R. 2454, as well as how that cost would be spread among households with different levels of income. The analysis does not include the effects of other aspects of the bill, such as federal efforts to speed the development of new technologies and to increase energy efficiency by specifying standards or subsidizing energy-saving investments.

Reducing emissions to the level required by the cap would be accomplished mainly by stemming demand for carbon-based energy by increasing its price.

The Expected Changes to Household Costs

Reducing emissions to the level required by the cap would be accomplished mainly by stemming demand for carbon-based energy by increasing its price. Those higher prices, in turn, would reduce households' purchasing power. At the same time, the distribution of emission allowances would improve households' financial situation. The net financial impact of the program on households in different income brackets would depend in large part on how many allowances were sold (versus given away), how the free allowances were allocated, and how any proceeds from selling allowances were used. That net impact would reflect both the added costs that households experienced because of higher prices and the share of the allowance value that they received in the form of benefit payments, rebates, tax decreases or credits, wages, and returns on their investments.

The incidence of the gains and losses associated with the cap-and-trade program in H.R. 2454 would vary from year to year because the distribution of the allowance value would change over the life of the program. In the initial years of the program, the bulk of allowances would be distributed at no cost to various entities that would be affected by the constraint on emissions. Most of those free allocations would be phased out over time, and by 2035, roughly 70 percent of the allowances would be sold by the federal government, with a large share of revenues returned to households on a per capita basis. This analysis focuses on the effect of the legislation in the year 2020, a point at which the cap would have been in effect for eight years (giving the economy time to adjust) and at which the allocation of allowances would be representative of the situation prior to the phase-down of free allowances. The incidence of gains and losses would be considerably different once the free allocation of allowances had mostly ended. Although the analysis examines the effects of the bill as it would apply in 2020, those effects are described in the context of the current economy—that is, the costs that would result if the policies set for 2020 were in effect in 2010.

In the initial years of the program, the bulk of allowances would be distributed at no cost to various entities that would be affected by the constraint on emissions.

On that basis, the Congressional Budget Office (CBO) estimates that the net annual economy-wide cost of the cap-and-trade program in 2020 would be $22 billion—or about $175 per household. That figure includes the cost of restructuring the production and use of energy and of payments made to foreign entities under the program, but it does not include the economic benefits and other benefits of the reduction in GHG emissions and the associated slowing of climate change. CBO could not determine the incidence of certain pieces (including both costs and benefits) that represent, on net, about 8 percent of the total. For the remaining portion of the net cost, households in the lowest income quintile would see an average *net benefit* of about $40 in 2020, while households in the highest income quintile would see a *net cost* of

$245. Added costs for households in the second lowest quintile would be about $40 that year; in the middle quintile, about $235; and in the fourth quintile, about $340. Overall net costs would average 0.2 percent of households' after-tax income. . . .

The Net Economy-Wide Cost

Taking into account the gross cost associated with complying with the cap ($110 billion); the allowance value that would flow back to U.S. households ($85 billion), both in the form of direct relief and indirectly through allocations to businesses and governments (all of which would eventually benefit households in people's various roles as consumers, workers, shareholders, and taxpayers); and the additional transfers and costs . . . (providing net benefits of $2.7 billion), the net economy-wide cost of the GHG cap-and-trade program would be about $22 billion—or about $175 per household. Four factors account for that net cost:

- the purchase of international offset credits (about $8 billion),
- the cost of producing domestic offset credits (about $3 billion),
- the resource costs associated with reducing emissions (about $5 billion), and
- the allowance value that would be directed overseas (about $6 billion).

Each of those components represents costs that would be incurred by U.S. households as a result of the cap-and-trade program but would not be offset by income resulting from the value of the allowances or from additional payments (such as increases in Social Security benefits) that would be triggered by the program.

Transitional Costs Will Balance Out for U.S. Households

The measure of costs described above reflects the costs that would occur once the economy had adjusted to the change in the relative prices of goods and services. It does not include the costs that some current investors and workers in sectors of the economy that produce energy and energy-intensive goods and services would incur as the economy moved away from the use of fossil fuels. To be sure, increased production of energy from non–fossil fuel sources (such as wind or solar) and a shift to more energy-efficient production processes would create jobs and profit opportunities as well. However, those jobs might be in different regions of the country or require different skills than the jobs being lost, and the profit opportunities might arise from different types of capital; their availability would mute but not eliminate the costs of the transition. Thus, investors would see the value of some stocks decline, and workers would face higher risk of unemployment as jobs in some sectors were eliminated. Stock losses would tend to be widely dispersed among investors because shareholders typically diversify their portfolios. In contrast, the costs of unemployment would probably be concentrated among relatively few households and, by extension, their communities. The magnitude of those transitional costs would depend on the pace of emission reductions, with more rapid reductions leading to larger costs.

> *The allowance value ... would flow back to U.S. households ($85 billion), both in the form of direct relief and indirectly through allocations to businesses and governments.*

The magnitude of transitional costs would also be affected by international trade, especially for goods or services that embody large amounts of GHG emissions. The cost of producing such goods in the United States would rise under the cap-and-trade program, thereby disadvantaging producers of those goods relative to foreign competitors that did not face a similarly stringent program for reducing emissions. Although large segments of the U.S. economy either do not face significant foreign competition (for example, the electricity and transportation sectors) or involve trade with countries that have a cap-and-trade program (the European Union, for example), some important manufacturing industries, such as steel, face competition from countries that do not face the costs of such a system.

The prices of stocks in industries that would be expanding under a cap-and-trade program—such as renewable energy—could rise, as would job openings in those industries.

With the Loss of Some Job Sectors, Others Will Grow

At the same time, as already noted, the prices of stocks in industries that would be expanding under a cap-and-trade program—such as renewable energy—could rise, as would job openings in those industries. CBO expects total employment to be only modestly affected by a cap-and-trade program to reduce GHG emissions. Except during cyclical downturns such as the current recession, most individuals who seek employment are able to find jobs, and a cap-and-trade program would not greatly diminish that ability. Some regions and industries would experience substantially higher rates of unemployment and job turnover as the program became increasingly stringent. That transition could be particularly difficult for individuals employed in those industries (such as the coal industry) or living in those regions (such as Appalachia).

However, any aggregate change in unemployment would be small compared with the normal rate of job turnover in the economy.

Cap and Trade Will Be Costly for Consumers, but It Is the Best Option for Reducing Carbon Emissions

Neal Dikeman

Neal Dikeman is a partner in Jane Capital Partners LLC, a merchant and investment banking firm focused on energy and environmental technology.

In ... the debate over Waxman-Markey [a cap-and-trade bill in the U.S. Congress], I think it's worth laying out some of the key debating points on how cap and trade works and why it's been our weapon of choice to date in the climate change fight.

I like to think of our carbon and energy problem as follows. We built the first industrial economies and long-term economic growth model in all of human history in the last 200 years on a cheap, available energy base, in part by effectively running down our existing inventories of energy stocks from the least cost to the most expensive. We now need a lot more inventory each year (since we've been successful and are a lot bigger), and we're into the expensive layer of our inventory, so it's hitting our global cost of goods heavier than before. And we know we need to find more sources to replenish inventories, and we know that if we move immediately to higher cost sources we'll pay the price in GDP [gross domestic product, a country's total economic output].

We also know that producing and using those inventories had a non-zero (and we argue about the level) cost to our environment that we have not measured well, but have been

Neal Dikeman, "Cap and Trade: How it Works and Why It Has Been the Option of Choice," *www.cleantechblog.com*, July 19, 2009. Reproduced by permission of the author. http://www.cleantechblog.com/2009/07/cap-and-trade-how-it-works-and-why-its.html.

working on reducing for the last three decades. But we've now run into a new part of that cost with carbon or GHGs [greenhouse gases] that's very large, and is going to take a much larger and bigger hit to take care of, and depending on your view, has an aggressive time fuse on it. Essentially this means pricing carbon into our economy, which will basically add a whole new cost in all of our supply chains, a cost that varies from country to country and industry to industry, and will shake up comparative advantage in trade. And because it's global, as far as the environment is concerned, for carbon, unlike most environmental pollutants, it doesn't matter where in the world it's emitted or reduced. So our problem is China's problem is Europe's problem is our problem.

We built the first industrial economies and long-term economic growth model in all of human history in the last 200 years on a cheap, available energy base.

The Goals Should Include Growth

So we start with a first climate change goal: to reduce the carbon emissions levels in the economy, by a level that we all debate by a point in time that we all debate. But we have to realize that while we do this, we do need to replace those energy supply inventories to both keep us where we are in GDP, and find new ones to sustain growth, or we'll solve our GHG problem simply by being really poor. And we have to remember that adding costs has to be paid for, and it isn't "business" that pays for it, it's us, with business as our proxy.

So my corollary is the goal should be to squeeze carbon emissions out of the global economy in the fastest, least costly path, and as fairly as possible. Sorting out what that means and how to do so is the rub. But part of fair should mean a "do no harm" principle for the economy as well as the environment—meaning that when we start, as far as possible no country or group or industry or company within industries gets penalized out of the gate without either compensation or enough time to adjust. Think of it like eminent domain. If we give something up to the greater good, we deserve to get paid for it.

Carbon taxes have big drawbacks. You can't be sure you'll actually get the level of reductions you want, because the tax fixes price, not volume.

We have two main ways to go about it, place a tax or penalty on the emissions, or constrain the emissions factors (like power generation, driving, etc.) Cap and trade is essentially a hybrid of the two. The cost of such carbon reduction, because of the ubiquitous nature of carbon, and typically inelastic demand curves for most energy and carbon intensive products, is spread across all consumers in any scenario, but depending on system design can be borne disproportionately by some groups, industries or countries. Our special challenge is because of that global nature, we literally *have* to have a solution that can engage and work in every country. Unlike cleaning up a local toxic spill, where we can fix ours without our trading partners, in carbon, if China fails, we fail. So if we try and succeed, and China does not try, the environment loses, and we lose worse. . . .

The Two Unlikely Options

Basically with carbon tax the government picks a series of carbon intensive industries or products, assigns a carbon value to them by one of a number of methods, and levies a tax on them. It's often touted by economists as theoretically the cheapest method, and generally an industry favorite because they know how much they'll have to pay and can plan.

But carbon taxes have big drawbacks. You can't be sure you'll actually get the level of reductions you want, because the tax fixes price, not volume. Worse, carbon is a global problem, and getting global tax codes to mesh together is virtually impossible (we can't even do it inside the United States), which means we may end up with everybody paying a different price of carbon and a complete mess. That certainly would throw the efficiency argument out the window. The next big disadvantage is that if you don't get the tax level and structure exactly right, businesses and consumers get hurt in unpredictable ways, and have little room to adjust if we get it wrong. So while theoretically better, it's not a very "fault tolerant" plan.

Main advantage is that you have a known cost to industry (which is why most industry prefers tax to trade or command and control). Next main advantage is that the government gets lots and lots of revenue, which is why many politicians favor it.

The second option is classic environmental "command and control," if you'll excuse the pejorative sounding nature of that term. Essentially the EPA [Environmental Protection Agency] or equivalent simply regulates everyone who produces GHGs, and tells them how much they can produce through a permitting process.

Cap and trade is the middle ground.

The advantage is that you know exactly how much emissions reduction you are going to get. The disadvantage is that you may pay much more than you thought, and sink your economy, especially if your trading partners are more lax on either regulation or enforcement, and you let the EPA pick the winners and losers. The other disadvantage is that there is no upside. Under no circumstances will you ever get more reductions than you thought, unlike cap and trade, where done right, you may.

Cap and Trade Is the Practical Approach

Cap and trade is the middle ground (which is why it keeps coming up). With cap and trade, the system operator designates how many credits can enter the system and prints them like money. It then designates how many credits a company must turn in each year or period per unit of production (i.e., 0.5 tons/MWH [megawatt hours] of power produced), and penalizes or shuts down the company if they don't turn in enough to meet their obligation. So no more emissions from a regulated sector will occur than credits (often called allowances) exist.

Then the regulator decides whether to sell the credits to the industry that needs them, or to simply allocate them (often based on some measure of current production). Both methods have pros and cons, and in practice have nothing to do with environmental protection or the price of carbon (the total level of credits and the relative level of credits to demand sets that) and more with subsidizing one industry vs. another, or collecting revenue for the government.

Cap and trade . . . assures us that we will meet our target goals . . . but it allows industry the flexibility to figure how to meet them cheapest.

Finally, the regulator can let offset credits be produced from the remaining unregulated sectors (or from inside a regulated or "capped" sector if appropriate adjustments are made), and sold to the emitters (it simply adjusts the cap so that the total level is where we want it to be). The advantage of this is that the regulations can be phased in easier, and we get a more equal price of carbon.

And what happens is that in unregulated sectors any time potential reductions exist (e.g., a very inefficient emitter that could be shut down or run more efficiently), carbon developers pay up for the rights to the reduction, and that emitter finds it's more profitable to do the right thing. The downside is that it looks like emitters are getting a profit off emissions.

In reality, they are getting paid to reduce emissions for you and me, at just the right price.

Then emitters and financial parties buy and sell these credits from the government or each other or develop offset credits in a race to pay the least. And since the regulator starts reducing the number of credits it puts into the system, it's kind of like musical chairs—the slowest, most carbon inefficient company gets left out and has to shut down, or shifts to a lower carbon production in order to stay in business.

Cap and Trade Represents Give and Take

The main advantages of cap and trade: 1) it assures us that we will meet our target goals like command and control, 2) but it allows industry the flexibility to figure how to meet them cheapest (which is good for all of us), 3) it tells us what the real price (or cost) of carbon actually is, 4) it's better at equalizing the price of carbon so everyone pays the same across different industries and geographies, and 5) in practice it costs less and is easier to implement in a multi-country environment than command and control or tax.

Main disadvantages: It takes some time to get up and running and makes it look like (not really true) emitters are making money off it. Trust me, if they thought it was a profit center, they'd be all over it. The final disadvantage is it depends on the government operator to manage a market, something where we've had some good success, but can be susceptible to politics as usual.

All . . . options will be expensive, and will be paid for by you and me at some point.

In essence, you can think of cap and trade as a carbon tax with a tax rate that varies with the market (going up if industry is worse at producing carbon reductions than the government thought and down if they are better, and similarly going down when the economy is bad and we can't afford it and up when the economy is strong) and a tax base that is higher for emitters and emissions intensive industries than for those more efficient.

In any case, all three options need a lot of money spent on new technology and good measurement and verification. All three options will be expensive, and will be paid for by you and me at some point. And in practice, we are doing all three options to varying degrees right now.

Hybrid Cars May or May Not Be Worth the Extra Cost

Lauren DeAngelis

Lauren DeAngelis is a nonfiction filmmaker and an online writer/editor for U.S. News & World Report *and other publications.*

With gas prices inching past $4 per gallon [in the summer of 2008], you're probably cursing that thirsty SUV [sport-utility vehicle] or turbo-charged roadster in the driveway. But would purchasing a more fuel-efficient car actually be worth it? We've simplified things and done the math for you—but the answer is far from simple.

Because hybrids cost more than gasoline-powered models, it's not necessarily cost effective to buy one, even when taking into account the money you'll save on gas. But, if fuel costs continue to rise, the gas savings will make up the price difference—right? And what about conventional gasoline-powered models . . . is it worth it to go for the smaller, fuel-efficient vehicle instead of the one you have your heart set on? Keep reading to find out.

We're using an easy formula so that you can plug in your own figures. First, take the number of miles you drive in a year (we're using 15,000, which the EPA [Environmental Protection Agency] says is average) and divide it by the car's combined fuel economy (available at www.fueleconomy.gov) to calculate the number of gallons you'll use in a year. Then, multiply that number by the cost per gallon (we're using $3.96, the national average at press time, according to AAA) to calculate how much you'll spend on gas in a year. Do these first two steps for each of the two models you're comparing.

Lauren DeAngelis, "Is That Hybrid Worth It? Be Sure to Check Your Math Before Trading in Your Car for a Hybrid," AOL autos, June 11, 2008. Originally published on U.S. News Autos at usnews.com/cars. Reproduced by permission of the author.

To find out how many years it will take for a hybrid to pay for itself, divide the extra money you would spend buying the hybrid by the extra money you would spend on gasoline for the non-hybrid—et voilà!

Because hybrids cost more than gasoline-powered models, it's not necessarily cost effective to buy one, even when taking into account the money you'll save on gas.

To Have and to Hybrid

Based on today's gas prices, the Mercury Mariner Hybrid makes the most financial sense if you're deciding between a hybrid and its gasoline-only counterpart. The base model starts at only $1,750 more than the conventional Mariner and should pay for itself in gas savings in just a little over two years. The Saturn VUE Hybrid and Ford Escape Hybrid will each start earning their keep in about five years.

Hybrid sedans have better gas mileage than hybrid SUVs, but the sedans cost a lot more than their gas-only counterparts. For example, the Honda Civic Hybrid's 42.2 mpg [miles per gallon] average fuel mileage will save you $600 per year, but its base price is almost $7,600 more than the conventional Honda Civic. You would have to drive the Civic Hybrid for at least 12.5 years to start seeing a return on your investment.

Of course, we can't forget the most popular hybrid—the Toyota Prius. Compared to the Honda Accord, a midsize gasoline-only sedan that costs a bit less, the Prius should take less than a year to make up for the price difference and will save you an additional $1,000 in gas costs.

According to our calculations, the worst hybrid values are the GMC Yukon Hybrid, Chevrolet Tahoe Hybrid and Chevrolet Malibu Hybrid, which will each take at least 16 years to earn back the extra dollars they cost. In fact, the Yukon and Tahoe hybrids cost nearly $15,000 more than the conventional models. The Malibu Hybrid will only save about $168 per year on gas, an increase that won't easily make up for the hybrid's nearly $2,800 price jump.

The Malibu Hybrid will only save about $168 per year on gas, an increase that won't easily make up for the hybrid's nearly $2,800 price jump.

Sacrificing Needs and Wants for Gas Mileage

A lot of consumers are looking at fuel-efficient, gas-only cars to save on gas. While that's a good strategy, it pays to be realistic about how much you'll actually save. Sporty drivers may be thinking twice about buying that costly BMW 3 Series and considering the 32 mpg MINI Cooper instead. The MINI will save you 10 miles per gallon, which translates to about $786 per year or $15.13 per week. Just make sure that $15 a week will make up for the MINI's much smaller interior and cargo area.

You may also be considering dropping a large SUV for a midsize model. Opting for the Honda Pilot instead of the Chevrolet Tahoe will save over $478 in fuel per year. Still, the annual gas savings come out to just $9.20 per week, which may not be enough to justify trading down. Likewise, the all-new Smart Fortwo's excellent 36 mpg average fuel economy saves $311 per year in gas compared to the Honda Fit. However, the yearly gas savings only translate to about $5.99 per week, which may not be worth the trade-off—especially when taking into account that the Smart requires premium fuel.

Even when you think two cars are similar, it can still pay—literally—to take a closer look. Choosing the Honda Civic over the Honda Accord will still get you seating for five and plenty of convenience features. But the Civic will only save

$273 per year on gas—$5.25 per week—so ask yourself if it's worth losing the Accord's sportier performance and nicer interior.

The Big Question

So, is going green worth it? The answer, as you may have learned by now, is that it all depends on what car you're buying. The key is to choose wisely, consider your options carefully, and always take time to do the math.

Consumers' Costs for Cap-and-Trade Legislation Are Grossly Underestimated

David W. Kreutzer, Karen Campbell, and Nicolas D. Loris

At the Heritage Foundation, a conservative think tank, David W. Kreutzer is senior policy analyst for energy economics and climate change, Karen Campbell is policy analyst in macroeconomics, and Nicolas D. Loris is a research assistant in the Thomas A. Roe Institute for Economic Policy Studies.

Last week [June 19, 2009], the Congressional Budget Office (CBO) released its analysis of the Waxman-Markey climate change bill [a cap-and-trade bill in the U.S. Congress] that had proponents of the bill claiming Americans could save the planet for just $175 per household. That was the figure CBO estimated cap and trade would cost households in 2020 alone.

Both the CBO's analysis and the subsequent legislation are troubled: The analysis grossly underestimates economic costs while the legislation will have virtually no impact on climate. Overall, there are a number of basic problems with CBO's analysis:

- their allowance cost numbers do not add up;

- they ignore economic costs such as the decrease in gross domestic product (GDP) as a result of the bill; and

- the analysis is an accounting analysis, not an economic analysis.

Problems with Costs and Distribution of Allowances

The CBO's June 19 study projected that the allowance price—the price to emit carbon dioxide—will be $28 per ton of CO_2 in 2020. Since there are 5.056 billion tons of CO_2 equivalent in the cap that year (the amount of carbon dioxide and other greenhouse gases businesses are allowed to emit), this projection implies a $141 billion gross cost; however, CBO lists the cost as $91.4 billion. Although there were no changes to the bill between June 5 and June 19, the CBO projected allowance revenues of $119.7 billion, $129.7 billion, $136 billion, $145.6 billion, and $152.9 billion for the years 2015–2019. As the cap on carbon dioxide becomes more stringent, one would expect the allowance revenue to continue to climb, not dramatically decrease to $91.4 billion.

The [Congressional Budget Office's] analysis grossly underestimates economic costs while the [cap-and-trade] legislation will have virtually no impact on climate.

The goal of a cap-and-trade program is to reduce the amount of carbon dioxide and other greenhouse gases in the atmosphere. In order to realize such reductions, cap-and-trade programs establish absolute limits on total emissions of greenhouse gases. Before businesses in a covered sector can emit a greenhouse gas, they need to have the ration coupons (also known as allowances) for each ton emitted. The price a firm pays for these allowances, euphemistically referred to as "climate revenue," should be considered tax revenue. CBO mistakenly assumes that the government spending and distribution of allowance revenue is the dollar-for-dollar equivalent to a direct cash rebate to energy consumers—that is, that the carbon tax is not a tax if the government spends the money, which is simply preposterous.

Ignoring Economic Pain

Most problematic is the CBO's complete omission of the economic damage resulting from restricted energy use. As footnote 3 on page 4 of the CBO analysis reads, "The resource cost does not indicate the potential decrease in gross domestic product (GDP) that could result from the cap. The reduction in GDP would also include indirect general equilibrium effects, such as changes in the labor supply resulting from reductions in real wages and potential reductions in the productivity of capital and labor." In the Heritage Foundation's analysis of the Waxman-Markey climate change legislation, the GDP hit in 2020 was $161 billion (2009 dollars). For a family of four, that translates into $1,870—a pretty big chunk of change that the CBO is ignoring.

> In the Heritage Foundation's analysis of the ... climate change legislation, the GDP hit in 2020 was $161 billion (2009 dollars). For a family of four, that translates into $1,870.

It is also worth noting that, of the 24 years analyzed by the Heritage Foundation's Center for Data Analysis (CDA), 2020 had the second lowest GDP loss. Furthermore, the CDA found that for all years, the average GDP loss was $393 billion, or over double the 2020 hit. In 2035 (the last year analyzed by [the] Heritage [Foundation]) the inflation adjusted GDP loss works out to $6,790 per family of four—and that is before they pay their $4,600 share of the carbon taxes. The negative economic impacts accumulate, and the national debt is no exception. The increase in family-of-four debt, solely because of Waxman-Markey, hits an astounding $114,915 by 2035.

An Accounting Analysis, Not an Economic One

The CBO analysis is an accounting analysis of the flow of allowance revenue; it is not an economic analysis of the true opportunity cost of the bill. The analysis's "net cost" is essentially the cost of producing offsets and other emissions reductions—a process similar to a company's chief financial officer doing a cash-flow analysis of one investment project. The CBO does not take into account the dynamic general equilibrium consequences of the much higher energy prices: There are serious economic impacts from the energy price increases that they ignore.

The CBO and Congress seem to assume that energy price increases can be mitigated by giving allowance revenue back to businesses and consumers. This is not how the economy works. Prices are merely an information signal about the relative scarcity of real resources that are being used. For example, if farmers use their land, labor, and equipment to produce offsets, instead of planting more food crops, the price of food will go up. Yet the CBO report ignores this reality.

The CBO analysis cannot be used to debate the economic cost versus economic benefit of the bill. Instead, it can be used only to follow the money of the allowance revenue so policy makers and the public can understand exactly how that piece of the legislation is being handled. There is value in keeping an accounting of this revenue flow in order to determine who is getting what, but CBO should make it clear that this is the limit of their analysis.

The CBO analysis . . . fails to take into account all the adverse effects that will ripple through the U.S. economy if cap and trade becomes law.

It is inappropriate to go beyond this analysis, for example, by comparing CBO's cost estimates to those of the Heritage

Foundation, the National Black Chamber of Commerce, or even the EPA [Environmental Protection Agency], as many members of Congress are already doing. These members are simply trying to compare two different cost concepts—accounting versus economic. Although the EPA's analysis is flawed for other reasons, mostly because of unrealistic assumptions, they at least attempt to estimate the economic cost, which the CBO did not.

Higher Taxes and Economic Devastation in Return for . . . Nothing?

Regardless of the CBO's cost estimates of the Waxman-Markey cap-and-trade program, the necessary second part of the question—what benefits do the costs generate?—remains unanswered. Americans will get almost nothing in exchange for these higher taxes, and the legislation will provide nothing for future generations except more debt and less economic opportunity. According to climatologist Chip Knappenberger, Waxman-Markey would moderate temperatures by only hundredths of a degree in 2050 and no more than two-tenths of a degree at the end of the century. This does not sound like a great deal for the next generation—millions of lost jobs, trillions of lost income, 50–90 percent higher energy prices, and stunning increases in the national debt, all for undetectable changes in world temperature.

The CBO analysis of Waxman-Markey fails to take into account all the adverse effects that will ripple through the U.S. economy if cap and trade becomes law. CBO's grossly underestimated costs mean members of Congress will be grossly misinformed when voting on the legislation.

Cap-and-Trade Legislation Is a Convoluted Scheme to Impose a New Tax on American Families

David Harsanyi

David Harsanyi is an editorial page columnist for the Denver Post, *an American newspaper.*

If you have even a basic grasp of cap-and-trade policy, you're one in a million.

According to a recent Rasmussen poll, given a choice of three options, only 24 percent of voters could even identify that cap-and-trade policies had anything to do with environmental issues. A higher number believed that it was about regulating Wall Street. A plurality had no idea what it was at all.

Who can blame them? It's preposterously convoluted.

And that's precisely the kind [of] confusion the backers of cap-and-trade schemes are counting on.

When it comes to environmental policy, politicians will rely on your good intentions on the issue and not much else. With cap and trade, however, the economic trade-offs are so damaging, the environmental benefits so negligible, and the plan such a clutter, that selling it—even to Democrats—is turning out to be difficult.

No Reduction of Emissions

The cap-and-trade bill being rammed through Congress by Henry Waxman, D-Calif., and Ed Markey, D-Mass., aims to dramatically reduce carbon dioxide emissions by making greenhouse gas emitting businesses purchase or trade government rationed or auctioned coupons in a "market."

Now, while most markets will trade commodities that are actually worth something, this artificial market would effectively nationalize the energy industry. And like any huge economic undertaking, it would be highly susceptible to fraud, insider trading, political influence, and every other ugly consequence of big government and big business getting cozy.

We can turn to the failed European experience of cap and trade to understand how. As the *New York Times* reported in 2008, a comparable system in Europe "unleashed a lobbying free-for-all that led politicians to dole out favors to various industries, undermining the environmental goals. Four years later, it is becoming clear that system has so far produced little noticeable benefit to the climate—but generated a multibillion-dollar windfall for some of the continent's biggest polluters."

The trouble is that no matter what they call the cap-and-trade bill, it is a new tax.

Oh, and from 2000 to 2006, European emissions rates under the cap-and-trade policy *increased* by 3.5 percent. During that same time, U.S. emissions increased by 0.7 percent.

A New Tax

So why go through all that trouble when there is a straightforward way to bring about similar—and hopefully better—environmental results?

When Colorado proponents of cap and trade visited the editorial board at the *Denver Post*, I asked them why Congress couldn't simply affix a carbon tax on these corporations. One reason, they admitted, was that there was no public appetite for a tax. (They failed to mention that cap and trade's tangled bureaucratic web would be nearly impossible to escape from once implemented, which I believe is the driving purpose of the bill.)

This cap-and-trade scheme would cost the average household $1,218 extra a year.

The trouble is that no matter what they call the cap-and-trade bill, it *is* a new tax.

A recent study released by the Tax Foundation contends that the cap-and-trade bill is a regressive tax on families, as the bottom 20 percent of income earners would pay 6.2 percent of their income toward the tax while the top 20 percent of income earners will pay 1.4 percent.

The report estimates that on average, this cap-and-trade scheme would cost the average household $1,218 extra a year. (The Congressional Budget Office analysis estimates that cap and trade would cost the average American family $1,600; others contend it would be even higher.)

Even if you believe such estimates are inflated, or that such sacrifices are worth it, wouldn't you, at the very least, expect results?

Martin Feldstein, a Harvard economics professor writing in the *Washington Post*, stated the "proposed legislation would have a trivially small effect on global warming while imposing substantial costs on all American households."

Feldstein points out that our share of global CO_2 [carbon dioxide] emissions is now less than 25 percent—and, because of other growing economies, in a percentage decline. Yet, a 15 percent drop in CO_2 output at home—if it happens—would only lower global carbon output by less than 4 percent. The cost for such a negligible improvement would make little sense.

You will, of course, hear the argument that doing *anything* is better than doing nothing. The problem is that's not the choice we face—and cap-and-trade proponents know it.

CHAPTER 4

What Is the Future for the Green Movement?

Chapter Preface

The U.S. environmental movement has historically been made up mostly of secular activists who relied on science as the basis for their defense of the environment. In recent years, however, observers have noticed a growing new trend of religious groups becoming more active in environmental efforts. In fact, according to a 2004 survey by the Pew Forum on Religion & Public Life, a nonpartisan research group, a fairly strong consensus on environmental policy exists among various faiths. The Pew report found that respondents in the survey, by a two-to-one margin, supported strong regulations to protect the environment, even if those regulations would result in job losses and higher consumer prices.

According to the Pew survey, more conservative religious groups (such as evangelical Christians, mainline Protestants, and Roman Catholics) and some racial minorities were less likely to back environmental policies while more modernist Christians, Jews, and secular Americans scored the highest in their support for the environment. Yet even some evangelical religions are wading into the environmental debate today. For example, a group called the National Religious Partnership for the Environment, an association of faith groups that includes both Catholics and evangelicals, launched an anti-SUV (sport-utility vehicle) campaign in 2002 called "What Would Jesus Drive?" The goal of the campaign was to encourage Americans to give up big, gas-guzzling vehicles in favor of more energy-efficient vehicles. Years earlier, the same group organized an effort to save the Endangered Species Act.

For pro-environment religious groups, protecting the environment is an act of faith—a position that is required by the Bible and theology. In the book of Genesis, for example, God instructs Adam, "Be fruitful and multiply, and fill the earth, and subdue it; and rule over the fish of the sea and over the birds of the sky, and over every living thing that moves on the earth." Based on this and similar teachings, religious environmentalists argue that because God created everything and gave mankind stewardship over the earth, humans have a responsibility to care for the environment and protect it from destruction. Many theologians have been making this point for years, but now it is being embraced by religious leaders and congregations.

An opposite interpretation of religious teachings—the idea that God gave humans dominion over the earth and the right to use its resources for industry and other human purposes, regardless of the damage this causes, appears to be losing favor in many religious groups. Rather, the pro-environment stance is that while God gave humans a right to use the earth and its creatures for their benefit, that dominion includes a responsibility to care for the environment.

Some observers see this religious environmental uprising as a boon to the green movement's hopes for a transformation to a more sustainable economy and world. Some commentators have even compared it to the battle against slavery, which benefited greatly from the involvement of churches and religious groups across the nation—groups that saw slavery as a sin against God's teachings. Today churches, temples, and synagogues are similarly recognizing the environment as a moral concern, preaching a form of faith-based environmentalism known as "Creation Care"—the simple idea that God requires people to take care of the environment and all its creatures. If widespread religious zeal can mobilize millions of Americans as allies in the environmental movement to demand changes in the way industry and agriculture manage the environment, many environmental activists say the result can only be positive.

On the other hand, a few scientists and activists worry that mixing religion and environmentalism could be dangerous. These critics argue that environmental efforts depend on rational, scientific analysis of the impact of various human activities, such as the use of pesticides and chemicals, while religion is essentially a belief that relies solely on faith. Their concern is that religion-based environmentalism could turn into an anti-technology, anti-industrial movement that could reject needed scientific, industrial, and economic progress. Many religious leaders say this should not be a concern, although they warn that doing business as usual, without regard for the environment, cannot continue.

Whatever the outcome of this growing religious concern about the environment, it is clear that the future of the green movement could be significantly affected by religious groups and faith-based environmental efforts. The authors of the viewpoints in this chapter focus on other possible directions the green movement might take in coming years.

The Green Movement Must Articulate a Vision for a Positive Green Future

Joel Makower

Joel Makower is a journalist and strategist on green business, technology, and marketing.

There's long been a fundamental problem with the green world—the myriad companies, activists, evangelists, politicians, clergy, thought leaders, and others who, each in their own way, have prodded us to address our planet's environmental ills. And it explains why, after four decades of the modern environmental movement, only a relative handful of companies and citizens have joined in, while many more have dragged their heels to slow, or even reverse, environmental progress.

The Need for a Green Vision

The problem is this: No one has created a vision of what happens if we get things right.

That seems odd, when you think about it. We have a crystal clear picture of the consequences of getting things wrong (thank you very much, [former vice president] Al Gore). We know well the potential devastation of unmitigated environmental problems: the droughts, floods, hurricanes, tsunamis, resource wars, famine, and pestilence. We know about epidemics of childhood asthma in inner cities, toxic rivers in impoverished lands, and depleted fisheries that may never fully recover. We see for ourselves the rampant development in formerly verdant landscapes. There are vivid pictures of denuded forests, strip-mined mountains, and strip-malled farmland.

Joel Makower, "Obama and the Vision Thing," *Joel Makower, www.makower.com*, January 10, 2009. Reproduced by permission of the author.

We read about these things, hear Hollywood stars fret over them, and may even experience them firsthand.

After four decades of the modern environmental movement, only a relative handful of companies and citizens have joined in.

Point is, we know what business as usual looks like.

But what about success? What happens if we get things right? What does *that* look like?

This, as much as anything, is a vision I'm hoping President [Barack] Obama can portray to America and the world. Yes, there is a list of necessary policy prescriptions as long as my arm (and, fortunately, a corps of green policy geeks much savvier than I who know how to get them enacted). But without the vision thing, even the best policies can only go so far.

This is no small matter. For decades, environmental leaders in business, activism, and government have expressed frustration that the public isn't behind them, except in disappointingly small numbers, despite a litany of increasingly dire environmental problems. These same leaders express bewilderment at the painfully slow uptake of green products and personal habits, from buying organics to recycling to energy conservation. Even when people understand the issues and consequences of everyday actions—the direct relationship between inefficient lightbulbs and the threat of global climate change, for example—they usually fail to act.

We've long known that fear is a limited motivator. Think of how persuasion has changed. A generation ago, we were told by advertisers to worry about ring around the collar, iron-poor blood, waxy yellow buildup, and the heartbreak of psoriasis. Madison Avenue believed that driving fear into the hearts and minds of the public would unleash a wealth of sales and profits. No longer. Today, profits come from imbuing visions of sexual appeal, personal freedom, and a life without worry. Those positive images are the ones that inspire people to take action and, for better or worse, make choices in the marketplace.

A Compelling Story

What is the positive image of "green" that will inspire a nation—indeed, the world—to transform itself in the way that Obama and others are hoping: that create jobs, build economic opportunities, engender energy independence, attack climate change, improve public health, reduce environmental degradation, and ensure national security?

We've long known that fear is a limited motivator.

Ask yourself: What does a world took like where former autoworkers and steelmakers are employed in well-paid jobs to manufacture turbines and solar panels, and where mechanics, electricians, truck drivers, and plumbers are working fervently to build the smarter, upgraded electricity grid needed to distribute all this homegrown energy? Where a new generation of smart buildings and electric vehicles are operating in concert on cheaper, less-polluting energy, and a new generation of technicians is needed to build and maintain them and infrastructure necessary to power them? Where every home, office, factory, and store is retrofitted or rebuilt to be as energy efficient as possible, made so by armies of newly trained workers from local communities? Where entrepreneurial companies are mining landfills in order to turn waste back into raw materials at a fraction of the cost and environmental impacts of mining or manufacturing new ones? Where food is grown and distributed regionally, reducing transportation emissions and ensuring food security, creating a wealth of jobs for local farmers, food processors, distributors, and others?

I could go on, but you get the point. It's a pretty compelling story. Who's telling it?

Precious few [people] can spin a positive, exciting story about a world in which thinking and acting green [cuts through] . . . economic, political, and social problems.

A Green Leader

Van Jones is. The author of *The Green Collar Economy[: How One Solution Can Fix Our Two Biggest Problems]* and one of my personal heroes, Jones may be the only one who has learned how to inspire people with the vision thing. And not just any people: Jones is providing hope to legions of the economic underclass who have largely been left out of the environmental movement to date. He's telling ghetto kids to "put down a handgun and pick up a caulking gun," and that "somebody's going to make a million dollars figuring out a way to get solar panels made and deployed in our hoods. I think it should be you." Another Jones classic line, about Obama: "It's not that we have a president who's black; it's that for the first time we have a president who's green."

Jones has the ear of Obama, [Speaker of the House of Representatives] Nancy Pelosi, and others, but beyond Jones, not many others have his vision or voice. Precious few others can spin a positive, exciting story about a world in which thinking and acting green becomes a pathway through the thicket of so many seemingly intractable economic, political, and social problems. And that lack of voices, itself, is a problem.

Can Obama incite and excite the populace by painting an enticing picture of a greener world? Of course: Yes, he can. But will he? Amid the many pressures he'll have—to cure an ailing economy, world strife, and, God knows, the common cold—will he be willing and able to place his political currency in the green vision thing? If he can, it could be one of the more profound exercises in the audacity of hope.

Without . . . vision, the notion of a greener economy is destined to be seen as a "nice to do," not a "need to do."

And what about the rest of us? What's the uplifting story each of us is willing and able to tell? How much of your own personal and professional currency are you willing to expend to help not merely portray this good, green vision but also to ensure it becomes reality?

The Risk of Failure

Without that vision, the notion of a greener economy is destined to be seen as a "nice to do," not a "need to do." It will be easily countered by the incumbent interests who hope to continue to profit from the existing model, and who will warn that this is no time to tinker with radical, untested ideas about how our world works. And our political leaders will follow the money, and the votes, watering down the green ideal until it becomes yet another tepid policy soup.

We've seen vividly what happens when presidents squander opportunities. After 9/11 [2001 terrorist attacks on New York and the Pentagon], President [George W.] Bush could have inspired Americans to demand energy independence as a means of avoiding future terrorist attacks, enacting a wealth of policy directives to promote more efficient buildings and vehicles and develop oil alternatives. He could have inspired us with a hopeful vision born of the tragedy we'd just endured. We would have swallowed . . . a dollar extra tax on gas, maybe more, knowing it was going to a worthy cause. But he told us to go shopping and left it at that. Eight long years later, we'll have another chance.

To quote Van Jones one more time: "Barack Obama helped us take America back. Now we have to help him take America forward."

African Americans Need to Be Included in the Green Agenda

John Kerry

John Kerry is a senator from Massachusetts and chairman of the Senate Committee on Foreign Relations.

For too long, most pundits have talked about the environment as, to borrow a phrase, a "white man's burden." Conventional wisdom has portrayed environmental justice as a pet project of beach cleaners, trail hikers, spotted owl savers and—worst of all—elitists.

But here's the reality: In the fight to save the environment, city dwellers, especially African Americans, have the most at stake. Today, African Americans are 79 percent more likely than whites to live in neighborhoods with the highest levels of industrial pollution. They are five times as likely to live within walking distance of a power plant and twice as likely to suffer lead poisoning. African American children are three times as likely to die of asthma-related causes. To anyone familiar with injustice in America, it's an all-too-familiar story: Pollution hurts everyone, but it hurts African Americans the most.

Today, African Americans are 79 percent more likely than whites to live in neighborhoods with the highest levels of industrial pollution.

The same is true of climate change. While we cannot know to what extent Hurricane Katrina's destructiveness was fueled by global climate change, we do know that climate change will bring more disastrous hurricanes just like it. We also know that after Katrina, those who lacked the money and mobility to escape were overwhelmingly black. Climate change will mean rising sea levels, more sweltering heat waves, and new and dangerous diseases. And, if history is any judge, many of the worst affected—and least able to escape—won't be white.

Green Pioneers

Thankfully, there are activists who have helped draw the connection between the environment and other, more traditional social issues. Van Jones, a civil rights attorney in Oakland, realized that the clean energy sector could eventually employ hundreds of thousands of inner-city residents. His book, *The Green Collar Economy[: How One Solution Can Fix Our Two Biggest Problems]*, was a best seller, and he's now a special adviser to President [Barack] Obama.

In 1997, Majora Carter began her career as a community activist by organizing protests against Mayor Rudy Giuliani's plan to install a waste transfer station in her South Bronx neighborhood. Her organization has secured over $30 million to revitalize the borough's landscape—and its economy—with a 23-mile "greenway."

And of course, there is Lisa [P.] Jackson, who in January of 2009 became the first African American head of the EPA [Environmental Protection Agency]. Before joining the Obama administration, Jackson was New Jersey's commissioner for environmental protection, where she proved that a tough administrator can use environmental law to save African American lives. She pushed for tough new legislation against the trucks and ships that ruined Newark's air quality, and she led over 1,000 compliance investigations in Camden and Paterson, cities that had been ignored by previous commissioners.

These pioneers have made great strides, but too many purveyors of conventional wisdom still treat the environmental justice movement as if it exists only in national parks and old-growth forests.

The Changing Environmental Movement

The good news is that Americans of all walks of life understand what the pundits overlooked—and they are already changing the face of the environmental movement. Today, a lot of Americans who care about the environment don't even think of themselves as "environmentalists" because a lot of money has been spent to brand the word as negative and define them as unrealistic or extreme.

Without environmental justice, social justice will never be complete.

The new environmentalists are farmers, ranchers, mothers, fathers, evangelical Christians, and bottom-line business people. They range from the CEO [chief executive officer] of Wal-Mart—who recently endorsed a mandatory cap on carbon emissions—to a retired commercial fisherman in North Carolina who began suffering from the same symptoms as the poisoned fish he caught in a river polluted by a nearby hog farm. They are fighting small but significant battles across America to reclaim the environment. Our challenge is to go to the grassroots and make sure the new environmentalists are African Americans, too.

How have we let such a distorted picture take hold? Part of the blame lies with the media: Any time a story about the environment does not mention the work of urban activists, a journalist has missed an important part of the picture.

But the biggest part of the blame, and the biggest part of the solution, lies with us. As citizens and activists (and sometimes as senators), it isn't always easy to connect the dots, but we can't afford not to. We must remember that cities are ecosystems and that global climate change exacerbates local poverty.

There is an often-repeated quote by one of America's first great naturalists, John Muir: "When we try to pick out anything by itself, we find it hitched to everything else in the universe." Muir died almost a century ago, but his words have never been more relevant.

When we talk about "the environment," we're talking about redwoods in northern California, but we're also talking about drinking water in east Baltimore. We're talking about ice caps melting at the North Pole, but we're also talking about levees breaking in New Orleans.

It is time for more community activists to be invited to connect the dots. Without environmental justice, social justice will never be complete.

Green Technology Will Create Economic Opportunity

Associated Press

Associated Press is an American news agency that distributes news and information to newspapers and broadcasters around the world.

Venture capitalist John Doerr made his name and fortune with early investments in Netscape Communications Corp., Amazon.com Inc., Google Inc. and other pioneering tech firms that went from scrappy start-ups to household names.

Now Doerr and his firm, Kleiner Perkins Caulfield & Byers, are placing big bets on an emerging sector he calls "green technology," one he believes could become as lucrative as information technology and biotechnology.

Kleiner Perkins, based in Menlo Park, California, plans to set aside $100 million of its latest $600 million fund for technologies that help provide cleaner energy, transportation, air, and water. That's on top of more than $50 million Kleiner Perkins had already invested in seven greentech ventures.

"This field of greentech could be the largest economic opportunity of the 21st century," Doerr said. "There's never been a better time than now to start or accelerate a greentech venture."

This field of greentech could be the largest economic opportunity of the 21st century.

As one of Silicon Valley's most respected investors, Doerr's decision to champion green technology as the next big thing is generating buzz in the venture capital community.

"Betting on a Green Future," *Associated Press*, April 11, 2006. Reprinted with permission of the Associated Press.

"When John Doerr talks, people listen," said Mark Heesen, president of the National Venture Capital Association. "John appears to have an innate ability to spot trends and execute a business plan that is actually able to take advantage of those trends."

Kleiner Perkins' plan to ramp up investment in green technology is just the latest sign of the sector's growth.

North American venture capitalists invested more than $1.6 billion in cleantech companies last year, a 35 percent increase over 2004, according to a report by the Cleantech Venture Network, a trade group.

"It's a strong area for venture capital," said Craig Cuddeback, the network's senior vice president, whose group expects venture capital investment in the sector to double over the next three years. "It's no longer a choice between whether you will be clean or profitable."

Investors are seeing better prospects as technologies advance, more seasoned entrepreneurs enter the field and cleantech companies generate higher revenue.

Also known as clean technology, the field includes technologies related to water purification, air quality, nanotechnology, alternative fuels, manufacturing, recycling and renewable energy.

As prices of more traditional energy sources continue to rise, the global market for clean energy sources such as biofuels, hydrogen fuel cells and solar and wind energy rose to $40 billion last year, according to a report released last month by Clean Edge Inc., a [California] Bay Area marketing firm. The figure is expected to more than quadruple to $167 billion by 2015, the report said.

Past investments in renewable energy and other clean technologies often resulted in disappointing returns, largely because the technologies and market demand weren't strong enough, Heesen said. Alternative energy firms must fight for their share of a market that's tightly regulated and dominated by the oil, coal and natural gas industries.

"There are a lot of obstacles that stand in the way of creating a new way of creating energy," Heesen said.

But investors are seeing better prospects as technologies advance, more seasoned entrepreneurs enter the field and cleantech companies generate higher revenue. Successful initial public offerings by cleantech companies, such as SunPower Corp. of Sunnyvale, California, and China's Suntech Power, have also stoked investor interest.

Besides investing in greentech ventures, Doerr said he and Kleiner Perkins plan to "advocate for policies that reduce the climate crisis and increase energy innovation."

Vinod Khosla, a Kleiner Perkins associate who recently started his own venture capital firm, is financing a California ballot initiative to fund alternative energy initiatives through tax hikes on oil companies.

Venture capitalists point to the global forces driving greentech investment: the rising cost of fuel; the economic expansion of China, India and other Asian nations; and growing worries over global warming.

"In my opinion, it's one of the most pressing global challenges we face," Doerr said. "It's causing the nations of the world to put an even higher priority than we have now on innovation."

Doerr sees another major trend: billions of people moving to cities in developing countries. Experts predict the number of people living in "megacities" with more than 10 million people will triple from 2 billion to 6 billion over the next 50 years, he said.

"This is the mother of all markets," Doerr said. "As those Asian economies rise, people will move from rural to urban settings. All those people will want the same things that you and I want—clean water, power and transportation."

Green-Collar Jobs Are the Future for the Next Generation Workforce

Wendy Priesnitz

Wendy Priesnitz is a journalist and book author who promotes sustainable practices in favor of social and ecological balance.

First of all, there is no finite definition of the term "green job" and the field is subject to its own style of greenwashing [exploiting the attraction to green business for profit]. Presumably, the term would refer to jobs that contribute to solving the climate change problem. It is most often used to describe positions in "natural" or "organic" (other problematic words) consumer products and services, renewable energy and environmental conservation. But as sustainability has become more popular, we see any job in those fields being called "green," including those such as administrative assistant, marketing representative and computer programmer, which require no special "green" training.

We think that's actually a good thing, since we all need to think green and every worker should be integrating sustainability practices into every job. It makes it difficult to sort out what is and isn't a green job, but perhaps that doesn't really matter!

We all need to think green and every worker should be integrating sustainability practices into every job.

The definition of "green-collar job" is a bit simpler, since it refers to the eco version of what we normally call "blue-collar

Wendy Priesnitz, "Are Green Jobs Really Green? (And How Do I Get One?)," *Natural Life*, May-June 2009, pp. 9–11. Copyright © 2009 Life Media. Reproduced by permission.

jobs." That means an auto assembly-line worker might become a wind turbine mechanic. And that person would obviously require special training.

There is a sense developing among some policy makers that to be truly green, a job must play a role in building a sustainable economy. And that includes not just environmental quality and general economic prosperity, but a reduction in poverty, inequality and discrimination. The 2008 *Green-Collar Jobs in America's Cities* report by Green for All and its partner, the Apollo Alliance, put it this way: "If a job improves the environment, but doesn't provide a family-supporting wage or a career ladder to move low-income workers into higher skilled occupations, it is not a green-collar job."

For instance, employment in industries such as recycling, waste management and biomass energy tends to be precarious and incomes low.

The Economic Crisis Could Increase Green-Collar Demand

The second issue is that there is a great deal of hype and even a lot of outright fiction around green jobs.

Assessments of the current availability of such jobs vary wildly and are often extremely optimistic. Nick Ellis, a managing partner at the San Francisco agency Bright Green Talent, says bluntly that there are few green jobs available right now and too few qualified candidates for them. However, it would appear that demand could increase quickly, given the efforts of a number of governments to solve the current economic crisis through spending on green infrastructure. The UNEP's [United Nations Environment Programme's] Green Jobs Initiative predicts that efforts to curb climate change will seed millions of new green jobs around the globe in the coming decades. According to its report *Green Jobs: Towards Decent Work in a Sustainable Low-Carbon World*, the global market for sustainable products and services is projected to double from $1.37 trillion to $2.74 trillion annually by the year 2020, with building and construction ranking among those sectors expected to have a significant environmental, economic and employment impact.

The problem for younger workers needing jobs now is that the transition to a green economy—as urgent as we all know it is—won't happen overnight. And the new green jobs will be replacing the huge number of blue (or should we say "brown") collar jobs that will be lost as governments and industry work to reduce greenhouse gas emissions and the auto industry adjusts to its new economic realities.

Some of the new jobs will be created in the renewable energy field—solar electricity, wind energy, geothermal and so on. People will be needed in the design, engineering, manufacturing and installation sectors, both residential and commercial. The energy efficiency field could present an even bigger job creation opportunity, since such measures offer the most benefit for the least cost and will therefore be the most popular among consumers. At the forefront of that trend are energy auditing, insulation and other types of renovations and retrofits.

Green Building and Transportation Bode Well for the Future

The green building industry will likely continue to grow, with green construction management becoming an important role. A recent survey conducted by McGraw-Hill Construction in partnership with the National Association of Home Builders, which found that more than one-fifth of builders said they'd be building ninety percent of their projects green by next year [2010]. The problem, of course, is that the housing industry is currently in a slump. But that bodes well for the future. Many more jobs will be created on the periphery of the actual construction industry. Organic and water-conserving landscaping jobs are also expected to increase, as are opportunities for nontoxic cleaning in both residential and commercial build-ings, hauling and reuse of construction materials and debris, and water efficiency technology.

Most of the evolving green careers are environmental twists on or new names for old professions, like law, ar-chitecture, product and packaging design, journalism, and urban planning.

Sustainable transportation is another sector that's bound to offer an increasing number of jobs—everything from bi-cycle repair and bike delivery services to public transit and de-sign, manufacturing and repair of alternative fuel vehicles.

Sustainable forest management could generate as many as ten million new green jobs internationally, according to the United Nations' Food and Agriculture Organization (FAO) in a statement earlier this year. Jan Heino, the deputy head of FAO's Forestry Department, says that "since forests and trees are vital storehouses of carbon, such an investment could also make a major contribution to climate change mitigation and adaptation efforts." New jobs could include forest manage-ment, agroforestry and farm forestry, improved fire manage-ment, development and management of trails and recreation sites, expansion of urban green spaces, restoring degraded for-ests and planting new ones.

The Green Evolution of Familiar Careers

Most of the evolving green careers are environmental twists on or new names for old professions, like law, architecture, product and packaging design, journalism, and urban plan-ning, as well as jobs in the eco-tourism industry.

Others examples of evolving green opportunities are engi-neering careers tied to research in renewable technologies like wind energy and alternative fuel production. A new branch of science called bio-mimicry uses nature as a model for solving engineering problems.

Emissions brokers will be in high demand if North America moves to a mandatory trading system for greenhouse gas emissions. Even the retail sector is opening up green jobs. Sears Canada, for instance, recently advertised opening for three sustainability manager positions at its head office. And Wal-Mart has invested heavily in greening itself as well.

Environmental journalist Joel Makower has his finger on the pulse of the green economy. In his online publication GreenBiz.com, he demonstrates that green jobs are not just a passing fad. He told *Forbes* magazine that there's a proven market, government backing and corporate buy-in for sustainability. And he says to expect green business and green careers to grow even more over the next decade as the economy recovers.

While waiting for the green jobs to multiply, . . . there are always opportunities to get some hands-on, real-world experience by volunteering with local sustainability projects.

In the meantime, job-specific training in the field of choice is a good career investment.

The growth in interest in green jobs means there is a comparable growth in green education and job training programs. Universities are adding green MBA [master of business administration] programs and offering other postgraduate degree programs, such as joint MBA/environmental science masters. And some are having a hard time keeping up with student demand. In Australia, 2008 applications for agriculture, environment and related studies increased one hundred and twelve percent over the previous year. In Canada, Dalhousie University has just announced a groundbreaking new undergrad cross-faculty program called Environment, Sustainability and Society, but that's just one of thousands of environmental courses available at universities and colleges these days.

Many institutions are making the environment a major focus and creating centers like York University's Centre for Applied Sustainability, Columbia's Earth Institute and the University of British Columbia's sustainability office, which is considered a North American leader. Such centers give students the chance to address environmental challenges through course work, research and hands-on involvement by greening their communities and their campuses.

Opportunities for Getting Your Foot in the Green Door

Much of the green-collar job training is happening at the college level, where programs are popping up like weeds in fields like renewable energy, building renovation and restoration, energy efficiency and natural building techniques. Organizations like Solar Energy International (SEI), a leader in solar energy education courses for close to twenty years, are another source of training. SEI is experiencing double-digit growth in the number of people interested in taking its classes due to the growth in the green market. LEED [Leadership in Energy and Environmental Design] training through the Canada or U.S. Green Building Council would be helpful if you're interested in the construction field.

And, finally, for those who see education as a holistic, life learning experience, there are alternatives to regular postsecondary programs. For instance, Living Routes, based in Amherst, Massachusetts, develops accredited, college-level sustainability programs based in ecovillages around the world.

While waiting for the green jobs to multiply, along with improving your education, there are always opportunities to get some hands-on, real-world experience by volunteering with local sustainability projects. Networking through initiatives like Green Drinks [a forum for green interests in cities around the world] or local environmental groups will also provide contacts for when positions open up that will help to improve the world.

The U.S. Congress Must Pass Cap-and-Trade Legislation to Move America into Clean Energy

Ed Perry

Ed Perry is the global warming outreach coordinator for the National Wildlife Federation, an environmental group.

In the upcoming months [in mid-2009], there will be considerable discussion about the president's [Barack Obama's] cap-and-trade program that will begin reducing the amount of carbon dioxide discharged into the atmosphere. Unfortunately, there is likely to be a lot more heat than light.

We will hear that cap and trade will break the budget, put people out of work, raise electricity rates and is nothing more than another tax.

Actually, cap and trade will be the single greatest mechanism that will move us to our new energy future. Without cap and trade, the fossil fuel industry can continue polluting the atmosphere for free. Paying for their pollution makes renewable energy such as solar, geothermal and wind power able to compete on a level playing field, one that is now greatly skewed toward the fossil fuel industry.

Cap and trade will be the single greatest mechanism that will move us to our new energy future.

Burning fossil fuels is precisely why we are having to deal with global warming, which climate scientists say is the greatest threat to human civilization that we have faced.

Ed Perry, "Cap and Trade: We Must Move Towards a Clean Energy Future," *Harrisburg Patriot News*, May 3, 2009. Reproduced by permission of the author.

The High Cost of the Status Quo

When we hear that cap and trade will raise our energy costs, or is a tax, we need to pay attention to the messenger. We have heard that line before, whenever the fossil fuel industry feels threatened. If it will raise costs, what should we compare those costs to? The status quo? Does anyone think that if we do nothing that energy costs are going to decline? We have already seen what doing nothing has done to energy costs.

During the Arab oil embargo of 1973, I sat in lines to buy gasoline at 38 cents/gallon. President [Richard] Nixon was so incensed that he embarked on . . . Project Independence, a plan that would free us from foreign oil by 1980. We all know where that went. At that time, we imported one-third of our oil. Today, with gas prices forecasted to go back above $3 [per] gallon, we import nearly two-thirds of our oil, and gas was at $4 [per] gallon last year [2008].

Families are paying higher and higher energy costs because we do not have a national energy policy to shift . . . to more dependable, cleaner alternatives.

During the last presidential election, we heard that the solution to our energy crises was drill, baby, drill. A report prepared by former President [George W.] Bush's Department of Energy [DOE] states that if we drilled everywhere in the Arctic National Wildlife Refuge, all along our coast, and on the 35 million acres the oil companies hold leases on out West, it would increase oil production by about 1.2 million barrels/day at peak production. The DOE said that would reduce the price of a barrel of oil by about $1.40, and lower the price of gasoline by 4–5 cents—by 2025!

A study by the Massachusetts Institute of Technology found that if we had passed the Climate Security Act last year, it would have reduced oil consumption by eight million barrels of oil per day by the year 2025. So what is the answer?

Drill in every conceivable location for 1.2 million barrels/day at peak production, or pass legislation that will reduce our consumption by eight million barrels/day?

The price of coal, and therefore electricity, also is going up. Electric bills in Pennsylvania are scheduled to go up by at least 50 percent in the next few years, and American Electric Power is trying to raise rates by 50 percent in Ohio and other Midwest states because coal is getting more expensive.

Our energy future lies in clean, renewable energy.

When we hear that cap and trade is a tax, what we are really hearing is an argument for maintaining the status quo. Families are paying higher and higher energy costs because we do not have a national energy policy to shift investments from oil and other dirty fuels to more dependable, cleaner alternatives.

Doing nothing has caused our electric bills to go up, our air quality to go down and the price of gas to go up. We continue to be held hostage by countries that don't like us.

A Clean Energy Future

Our energy future lies in clean, renewable energy. Making the fossil fuel industry pay for pollution will make the sun, geothermal and wind [energies] more economical and put millions of our fellow Americans back to work building our new energy system. What we need now is for our elected representatives to pass legislation, this year, that sets a declining cap on carbon dioxide emissions.

We need our legislators to get off the fence and lead us to our new energy future and a green economy that will provide millions of jobs in the renewable energy sector. We have been talking about developing an energy policy for as long as I have been driving. Now is the time to do it.

The World Must Figure Out How to Mesh Economic Development with Good Environmental Policies

Anne Applebaum

Anne Applebaum is a journalist, author, and columnist for both the Washington Post *and* Slate, *an online magazine.*

If you haven't done so already, meet the [Tata] Nano, possibly the most significant new car of the decade. Small, cute, and snub-nosed, it fits four people and a duffel bag, has a single windshield wiper, travels at 60 mph, and it's all yours for the princely sum of $2,500, roughly the same price as the DVD system in your neighbor's Lexus and about half the price of the cheapest cars on the market today.

Even better, at least for the philosophically minded, the Nano comes with its own moral conundrum: What happens when the laudable, currently fashionable movement to improve the environment comes directly into conflict with the equally laudable, equally fashionable movement to improve the lives of the poor?

By its very existence, the Nano, which is being launched in India, embodies this dilemma. Though the car will remain out of reach for the poorest, it's an obvious boon for those Indians just entering the middle class—and not just as a convenience. As Indians become more mobile, jobs will become more flexible, trade and commerce easier, growth even faster. "I hope this changes the way people travel in rural India," the manufacturer declared as the car was unveiled at the Delhi Auto Expo: "We are a country of a billion and most are denied connectivity."

Anne Applebaum, "The Nano Challenge: What Happens When the Green Movement Crashes into the Anti-Poverty Crusade?" *Slate*, January 14, 2008. Copyright © 2008 Washington Post, Newsweek Interactive Co. LLC. Reproduced by permission.

But if all goes according to plan, 250,000 Nanos will be manufactured in the first year of production, and those numbers will rise rapidly as production lines are opened in Africa, South America, and Southeast Asia. Though the small Nano uses less gasoline than many larger cars, the enormous potential numbers could mean an equally enormous environmental impact. Since it will be a long time before Nano drivers will be able to afford the $20,000-plus hybrids now on the market, let alone a Honda FCX Clarity, the prototype experimental hydrogen car thought to be worth as much as $10 million apiece, that means an exponential rise in carbon emissions as well as other kinds of pollutants. The United Nations' top climate scientist, Indian economist Rajendra Pachauri—chair of the Intergovernmental Panel on Climate Change, which shared the Nobel Peace Prize with Al Gore—has said he is already "having nightmares" about precisely this scenario.

There is still a vast disparity between the world of the cheap and mass-produced and the world of the exclusive and green.

The Disparity Between Green and Mass Production

What's true of cars is true of many other products: There is still a vast disparity between the world of the cheap and mass-produced and the world of the exclusive and green. Hershey's bars can be purchased online, in bulk, for 52 cents apiece; a 1.5-oz organic granola bar (containing organic goji berries, agave nectar, and Himalayan salt) will set you back $4.49. If you think that's a silly example (which, OK, it is), think about the organic produce now available in many supermarkets at higher prices. You may feel virtuous when you pay for it—I know I do—but it's not going to feed the masses.

What does feed the masses, at least at the moment, is no secret: high-tech farming, chemical fertilizers, genetically engineered crops. Modern means of communication and transport—cars, telephones, computers—will eventually make the poor richer, too. Though there are many fans of "environmentally sustainable development" who believe we can have less poverty, less pollution, and lower carbon emissions at the same time, that's not happening out there in the real world, as the unveiling of the Nano demonstrates well.

Fans of "environmentally sustainable development" . . . believe we can have less poverty, less pollution, and lower carbon emissions . . . [but] that's not happening out there in the real world.

I'm not making an ideological argument here or manufacturing an excuse for American super-consumers, with our HUMMERS and McMansions. I'm not offering a proper answer to the puzzle proffered above, unfortunately, just stating the rarely acknowledged facts: Probably there should be an emissions-free car available for $2,500 (or an organic granola bar for 52 cents), but, at the moment, there isn't. There must be a way to reconcile mass car ownership with global warming, but, at the moment, we haven't found it. There is no profound reason why good environmental policies have to come into conflict with economic growth, but, at the moment, they often do. In many countries, the desire not to be poor is, at the moment, stronger than the desire to breathe clean air. Look at photographs of Beijing in the smog if you don't believe me.

Maybe technology will save us. But in the meantime, the global conversation about climate change, environmental conservation, and fossil fuel consumption would become infinitely more interesting if the participants, particularly the ones dressed in organic haute couture, forthrightly acknowledged the real trade-offs. At the recent Bali conference on climate change, there was some talk of compensating developing countries for preserving their forests, as well as subsidies for clean technology. If, at the next conference, delegates also focus even a few minutes of their attention on the millions of Nano cars that will take to the roads in India and elsewhere over the next few years, then we'll know they're really serious.

A Low-Carbon Economy Will Create a Livable Future

Alok Jha

Alok Jha is a science and environment correspondent at the Guardian, *a British newspaper.*

A low-carbon economy will be the culmination of thousands of decisions by governments, businesses and individuals about how we choose to balance environment and economy. There isn't one correct future but many, with each detail in each country dependent on the will of its people.

One thing is certain, though. Anyone concerned about having to give up his modern lifestyle for an austere existence can rest easy. The big differences between now and the low-carbon future will not be the way the world looks or what we will be able to do in it, but how it is arranged.

The big differences between now and the low-carbon future will not be the way the world looks or what we will be able to do in it, but how it is arranged.

Clean Electricity

The biggest hurdle is electricity. Three-quarters of our global electricity needs come from burning fossil fuels. The low-carbon future will demand that none of that electricity emits carbon dioxide [CO_2]. So every gas or coal-fired power plant, of which there will be many in China and India, will have carbon-capture technology to trap and store CO_2 underground. Renewable sources including wind, tide, wave, and sun will, through investment in basic research in the coming decades, be commercially viable. Far from being forbidding installations belching out carbon dioxide, renewable power stations will be smaller, emit no CO_2 and tap into near-limitless supplies of free fuel.

Clean electricity will have a knock-on effect on the other modern carbon nasty—transport. When electricity is cheap and clean, there is no reason not to use its power as much as possible. Electric cars, buses, lorries [motortrucks] and high-speed trains will move us and our goods, yet make no contribution to global warming. Though mass public transport will be the travel mode of choice, personal cars will remain. You might not own one yourself, instead borrowing from clubs when needed. By planning towns around pedestrians and investing in cycle lanes, local councils will encourage travel under two miles to be under your own steam or by hydrogen buses.

The biggest hurdle is electricity.... The low-carbon future will demand that none of that electricity emits carbon dioxide.

Flying will be a problem. Improved aerodynamics, lighter aircraft and mixing biofuels into jet fuel will bring down the carbon cost of air miles. Carbon reductions in energy production and road transport will mitigate some of the rise in emissions from the growth in flights in China and India, but environmental campaigners will not be satisfied. Expect punishing taxes on plane tickets, tied to their carbon cost, to discourage flying unless there really is no alternative. In these situations, a personal carbon-rationing system, linked to national CO_2 emissions targets, will allow individuals to emit a certain amount of greenhouse gases into the atmosphere.

But the number of long journeys, particularly for work, will drop dramatically as high-speed Internet connections enable high-quality video conferences and easy communications for people on different sides of the world. Many people will stop commuting to their offices or factories, preferring to work from home.

A Culture of Reusing, Not Wasting

Homes might look the same, for nostalgic reasons, but will be fundamentally different. Bricks coated with solar paint will be held together with cement that soaks up CO_2 from the air around it. Triple-glazed windows will reduce the need for heating in winter and cooling in summer.

Only the most energy-efficient fridges and washing machines will be available to buy while LEDs [light-emitting diodes] in lamps and displays will turn electricity into light efficiently instead of wasting most of it as heat. Automatic controls will warm rooms only when needed and switch appliances and lights off when they're not needed.

Our throwaway culture will disappear. By encouraging people to re-use as much as possible, less waste will end up in landfills and the carbon in our possessions (the stuff emitted to make our clothes, toys or furniture) will not be wasted. Products will be made to last and, when they come to the end of their useful life, be repaired rather than thrown away. Packaging will be virtually nonexistent and, where it exists, will be recyclable or compostable.

People will use water more carefully. Rain will be collected from home and office rooftops and filtered using carbon-free electricity so that it is drinkable. Any water drained away in a building will be recycled and treated locally to wash clothes or flush toilets. Bottled water will be banned.

Food will come from local farms or factories to reduce the carbon cost of transport. Meat lovers, because of their high-carbon diets, will have to use up their personal carbon rations whenever they bite into a steak or else make sure their food comes from local, sustainable farms that produce meat artificially.

Locally produced electricity will also play a big part in keeping homes carbon free. Solar thermal panels, community-based combined heat and power plants running on carbon-neutral wood chips, micro wind turbines and ground source heat pumps mean that local districts won't need all their power from today's centralised power stations. Local heat and power networks could even feed into the national grid during times of great demand.

This is one of many visions for a low-carbon world in 2050. It seems a long way off and whether we get there depends on decisions made over the next few years.

The New Green Movement Will Upgrade Our Civilization

Alex Steffen

Alex Steffen is the executive editor of Worldchanging.com, a nonprofit Internet organization that champions environmental sustainability.

For decades, environmentalists have warned of a coming climate crisis. Their alarms went unheeded, and last year [2005] we reaped an early harvest: a singularly ferocious hurricane season, record snowfall in New England, the worst-ever wildfires in Alaska, arctic glaciers at their lowest ebb in millennia, catastrophic drought in Brazil, devastating floods in India—portents of global warming's destructive potential.

Green-minded activists failed to move the broader public not because they were wrong about the problems, but because the solutions they offered were unappealing to most people. They called for tightening belts and curbing appetites, turning down the thermostat and living lower on the food chain. They rejected technology, business, and prosperity in favor of returning to a simpler way of life. No wonder the movement got so little traction. Asking people in the world's wealthiest, most advanced societies to turn their backs on the very forces that drove such abundance is naive at best.

[Environmentalists in the past] rejected technology, business, and prosperity in favor of returning to a simpler way of life.

With climate change hard upon us, a new green movement is taking shape, one that embraces environmentalism's

Alex Nikolai Steffen, "The Next Green Revolution: How Technology Is Leading Environmentalism out of the Anti-Business, Anti-Consumer Wilderness," *Wired*, vol. 14, May, 2006. Reproduced by permission of the author.

concerns but rejects its worn-out answers. Technology can be a font of endlessly creative solutions. Business can be a vehicle for change. Prosperity can help us build the kind of world we want. Scientific exploration, innovative design, and cultural evolution are the most powerful tools we have. Entrepreneurial zeal and market forces, guided by sustainable policies, can propel the world into a bright green future.

A Commitment to Upgrading Civilization

Americans trash the planet not because we're evil, but because the industrial systems we've devised leave no other choice. Our ranch houses and high-rises, factories and farms, freeways and power plants were conceived before we had a clue how the planet works. They're primitive inventions designed by people who didn't fully grasp the consequences of their actions. Consider the unmitigated ecological disaster that is the automobile. Every time you turn on the ignition, you're enmeshed in a system whose known outcomes include a polluted atmosphere, oil-slicked seas, and desert wars. As comprehension of the stakes has grown, though, a market has emerged for a more sensible alternative. Today you can drive a Toyota Prius that burns far less gasoline than a conventional car. Tomorrow we might see vehicles that consume no fossil fuels and emit no greenhouse gases. Combine cars like that with smarter urban growth and we're well on our way to sustainable transportation.

With climate change hard upon us, a new green movement is taking shape, one that embraces environmentalism's concerns but rejects its worn-out answers.

You don't change the world by hiding in the woods, wearing a hair shirt, or buying indulgences in the form of save the earth bumper stickers. You do it by articulating a vision for the future and pursuing it with all the ingenuity humanity can muster. Indeed, being green at the start of the 21st century requires a wholehearted commitment to upgrading civilization. Four key principles can guide the way:

Renewable energy is plentiful energy. Burning fossil fuels is a filthy habit, and the supply won't last forever. Fortunately, a growing number of renewable alternatives promise clean, inexhaustible power: wind turbines, solar arrays, wave-power flotillas, small hydroelectric generators, geothermal systems, even bioengineered algae that turn waste into hydrogen. The challenge is to scale up these technologies to deliver power in industrial quantities—exactly the kind of challenge brilliant businesspeople love.

Efficiency creates value. The number one U.S. industrial product is waste. Waste is worse than stupid; it's costly, which is why we're seeing businesspeople in every sector getting a jump on the competition by consuming less water, power, and materials. What's true for industry is true at home, too: Think well-insulated houses full of natural light, cars that sip instead of guzzle, appliances that pay for themselves in energy savings.

Cities beat suburbs. Manhattanites use less energy than most people in North America. Sprawl eats land and snarls traffic. Building homes close together is a more efficient use of space and infrastructure. It also encourages walking, promotes public transit, and fosters community.

Quality is wealth. More is not better. Better is better. You don't need a bigger house; you need a different floor plan. You don't need more stuff; you need stuff you'll actually use. Eco-friendly designs and nontoxic materials already exist, and there's plenty of room for innovation. You may pay more for things like long-lasting, energy-efficient LED [light-emitting diodes] lightbulbs, but they'll save real money over the long term.

A Bright Future

Redesigning civilization along these lines would bring a quality of life few of us can imagine. That's because a fully functioning ecology is tantamount to tangible wealth. Clean air and water, a diversity of animal and plant species, soil and mineral resources, and predictable weather are annuities that will pay dividends for as long as the human race survives—and may even extend our stay on Earth.

It may seem impossibly far away, but on days when the smog blows off, you can already see it: a society built on radically green design, sustainable energy, and closed-loop cities; a civilization afloat on a cloud of efficient, nontoxic, recyclable technology. That's a future we can live with.

Organizations to Contact

The editors have compiled the following list of organizations concerned with the issues debated in this book. The descriptions are derived from materials provided by the organizations. All have publications or information available for interested readers. The list was compiled on the date of publication of the present volume; names, addresses, phone and fax numbers, and e-mail and Internet addresses may change. Be aware that many organizations take several weeks or longer to respond to inquiries, so allow as much time as possible.

The Alliance for Climate Protection

120 Hawthorne Avenue, Palo Alto, CA   94301
(650) 566-9730
e-mail: use online form
Web site: www.climateprotect.org

The Alliance for Climate Protection is a nonprofit educational organization, led by former vice president Al Gore, that seeks to persuade the American people (and people elsewhere in the world) of the importance and urgency of adopting and implementing effective and comprehensive solutions for the climate crisis. The group's Web site contains a News section that lists numerous news articles and press releases about recent legislative and other developments on the issues of clean energy and climate change.

Center for a New American Dream

6930 Carroll Avenue, Suite 900, Takoma Park, MD   20912
(301) 891-3683
e-mail: newdream@newdream.org
Web site: www.newdream.org

The Center for a New American Dream was founded in 1997 to address the environmental and social impacts of unsustainable consumption. The organization works to educate consumers about the environmental and health impacts of their purchases and encourage individuals and institutions to embrace greener choices. The group's Web site contains numerous tips for homes, workplaces, and the community.

Intergovernmental Panel on Climate Change (IPCC)

c/o World Meteorological Organization
7bis Avenue de la Paix, C.P. 2300, Geneva 2   CH-1211
   Switzerland
+41-22-730-8208/84
e-mail: IPCC-Sec@wmo.int
Web site: www.ipcc.ch/

The Intergovernmental Panel on Climate Change (IPCC) is a scientific body set up by the United Nations Environment Programme (UNEP) and the World Meteorological Organization (WMO) to provide decision makers around the world and others interested in climate change with an objective source of information about climate change. The IPCC's role is to assess on a comprehensive, objective, open, and transparent basis the latest scientific, technical, and socioeconomic literature produced worldwide that is relevant to the understanding of the risk of human-induced climate change, its observed and projected impacts, and options for adaptation and mitigation. This site provides access to each of the IPCC reports on climate change.

National Center for Policy Analysis (NCPA)

601 Pennsylvania Avenue NW, Suite 900, South Building
Washington, DC   20004
(202) 220-3082 • fax: (202) 220-3096
Web site: www.ncpa.org

The National Center for Policy Analysis (NCPA) is a nonprofit, nonpartisan public policy research organization that promotes private alternatives to government regulation and control and defends the competitive, entrepreneurial private sector. A search of the NCPA's Web site produces a list of articles and reports analyzing green initiatives from a conservative point of view. Examples of publications include "Green Jobs: Myths vs. Facts" and "Wind Power: Red Not Green."

National Wildlife Federation

11100 Wildlife Center Drive, Reston, VA   20190-5362
(800) 822-9919
Web site: www.nwf.org

The National Wildlife Federation is an organization that seeks to inspire Americans to protect wildlife. A search of the group's Web site for green topics produces a long list of articles and publications touching on many of the issues in the green movement. Examples include "Carbon Cap Must Be Clean, Green and Fair" and "Green Consumer."

Natural Resources Defense Council (NRDC)

40 West Twentieth Street, New York, NY   10011
(212) 727-2700 • fax: (212) 727-1773
e-mail: nrdcinfo@nrdc.org
Web site: www.nrdc.org

The Natural Resources Defense Council (NRDC) is an environmental action organization with 1.2 million members and online activists that seeks to protect the planet's wildlife and wild places and to ensure a safe and healthy environment for all living things. Its Web site contains special sections on green living and green business, which provide in-depth information about various aspects of the green movement.

Pew Research Center

1615 L Street NW, Suite 700, Washington, DC   20036
(202) 419-4300
e-mail: info@pewresearch.org
Web site: http://pewresearch.org

The Pew Research Center is a nonpartisan "fact tank" that provides information on the issues, attitudes, and trends shaping America and the world. It conducts public opinion polls and social science research, reports and analyzes news, and holds forums and briefings, but it does not take positions on policy issues. The center's Web site includes publications relevant to the green movement, including reports and news articles. Two examples are "Both Reds and Blues Go Green on Energy" and "Opinion: Green, Meet God."

Sierra Club

85 Second Street, 2nd Floor, San Francisco, CA   94105
(415) 977-5500 • fax: (415) 977-5799
e-mail: information@sierraclub.org
Web site: www.sierraclub.org

The Sierra Club is a well-known grassroots environmental organization based in the United States and founded in 1892 by the early environmentalist John Muir. The group publishes a magazine, *Sierra*, and its Web site contains a News section that leads researchers to various articles and publications on living green and related topics.

Sustainable Works

1744 Pearl Street, Santa Monica, CA   90405
(310) 458-8716
e-mail: info@sustainableworks.org
Web site: www.sustainableworks.org

Sustainable Works is a nonprofit environmental education organization funded by the City of Santa Monica's Sustainable City Plan to promote sustainable practices in businesses, colleges, and residential communities. The group's Web site describes programs that offer greening advice for residences, students, businesses, and communities.

Union of Concerned Scientists (UCS)

2 Brattle Square, Cambridge, MA   02238-9105
(617) 547-5552 • fax: (617) 864-9405
Web site: www.ucsusa.org

The Union of Concerned Scientists (UCS) is a leading science-based nonprofit organization working for a healthy environment and a safer world. The group's Web site contains sections on global warming, clean vehicles, clean energy, and other environmental topics.

Worldwatch Institute
1776 Massachusetts Avenue NW
Washington, DC 20036-1904
(202) 452-1999 • fax: (202) 296-7365
e-mail: worldwatch@worldwatch.org
Web site: www.worldwatch.org

Worldwatch Institute is an independent research organization that seeks to generate and promote ideas to empower decision makers to build an ecologically sustainable society that meets human needs. Worldwatch focuses on issues such as climate change, resource degradation, population growth, and poverty, and it publishes the bimonthly *World Watch* magazine, an annual report on the state of the environment called *State of the World*, and various other reports and papers. A search of its Web site for information on the green movement produces a list of relevant articles and publications.

World Wildlife Fund (WWF)
1250 Twenty-fourth Street NW, PO Box 97180
Washington, DC 20090-7180
(202) 293-4800 • fax: (202) 293-9211
Web site: www.worldwildlife.org

The World Wildlife Fund (WWF) is a multinational organization dedicated to conserving and protecting nature. The WWF Web site contains a wealth of information about environmental topics, including a special section on climate change that provides an overview of the issue, details the group's projects in this area, and contains information about what individuals, businesses, and governments can do to help.

Bibliography

Books

Jamal Ali

Black and Green: Black Insights for the Green Movement. Lanham, MD: Hamilton Books, 2009.

Brian Dumaine

The Plot to Save the Planet: How Visionary Entrepreneurs and Corporate Titans Are Creating Real Solutions to Global Warming. New York: Crown Business, 2008.

Andrés R. Edwards

The Sustainability Revolution: Portrait of a Paradigm Shift. Gabriola Island, BC, Canada: New Society Publishers, 2005.

Daniel Esty and Andrew Winston

Green to Gold: How Smart Companies Use Environmental Strategy to Innovate, Create Value, and Build Competitive Advantage. Hoboken, NJ: Wiley, 2009.

Thomas L. Friedman

Hot, Flat, and Crowded: Why We Need a Green Revolution—and How It Can Renew America. New York: Farrar, Straus and Giroux, 2008.

Paul Hawken

Natural Capitalism: Creating the Next Industrial Revolution. New York: Back Bay Books, 2008.

Jane Hoffman and Michael Hoffman — *Green: Your Place in the New Energy Revolution.* New York: Palgrave Macmillan, 2008.

Greg Horn — *Living Green: A Practical Guide to Simple Sustainability.* Topanga, CA: Freedom Press, 2006.

Huey D. Johnson — *Green Plans: Blueprint for a Sustainable Earth.* Lincoln, NE: University of Nebraska Press, 2008.

Van Jones with Ariane Conrad — *The Green-Collar Economy: How One Solution Can Fix Our Two Biggest Problems.* New York: HarperOne, 2008.

Joel Makower and Cara Pike — *Strategies for the Green Economy: Opportunities and Challenges in the New World of Business.* New York: McGraw-Hill, 2009.

William McDonough and Michael Braungart — *Cradle to Cradle: Remaking the Way We Make Things.* New York: North Point Press, 2002.

Steve Milloy — *Green Hell: How Environmentalists Plan to Control Your Life and What You Can Do to Stop Them.* Washington, DC: Regnery Publishing, 2009.

Lyndsay Moseley and the staff of Sierra Club Books, eds. — *Holy Ground: A Gathering of Voices on Caring for Creation.* San Francisco, CA: Sierra Club Books, 2008.

Ron Pernick and Clint Wilder — *The Clean Tech Revolution: The Next Big Growth and Investment Opportunity*. New York: Collins Business, 2007.

Richard Register — *EcoCities: Rebuilding Cities in Balance with Nature*. Gabriola Island, BC, Canada: New Society Publishers, 2006.

Jack Uldrich — *Green Investing: A Guide to Making Money Through Environment Friendly Stocks*. Avon, MA: Adams Media, 2008.

Periodicals

Jeffrey Ball — "Will the Developing World Risk Growth for Green?" *Wall Street Journal*, September 22, 2007. http://online.wsj.com.

Jonathan Bilyk — "Cap and Trade: Is It Worth the Cost?" *Chronicle* (Kane County, IL), July 18, 2009. www.kcchronicle.com.

Karen Breslau — "The Growth in 'Green-Collar' Jobs," *Newsweek*, April 8, 2008. www.newsweek.com.

Michael Burnham — "'New Urbanists' Look Backward in Bid to Trim Residential Energy Use, Pollution," Greenwire (E & E Publishing), February 20, 2007. www.eenews.net.

Ursula M. Burns — "Is the Green Movement a Passing Fancy? With a Struggling Economy and Lower Oil Prices, We'll Get to See How Committed to Green Technology Companies Really Are," *BusinessWeek*, January 27, 2009. www.businessweek.com.

Patricia Cecil-Reed — "The Best Jobs in America's Green Movement," Yahoo! HotJobs, 2009. http://hotjobs.yahoo.com.

Saheli Datta and Todd Woody — "8 Technologies for a Green Future," CNNMoney.com, March 7, 2007. http://money.cnn.com.

Olivia Gentile — "Out of the Wilderness: The Mainstream Green Movement Heads Toward People of Color," *Scientific American*, June 10, 2009. www.scientificamerican.com.

Chris Goodall — "The Green Movement Must Learn to Love Nuclear Power: The Public Debate About Energy Options Needs to Be Realistic," *Independent* (United Kingdom), February 23, 2009. www.independent.co.uk.

Van Jones — "Opportunities for Green Growth: Myths and Realities About Green Jobs," Center for American Progress Action Fund, January 15, 2009. www.americanprogressaction.org.

Anya Kaplan-Seem — "The Future of Green Building," *BusinessWeek*, March 16, 2009. www.businessweek.com.

Elizabeth Kolbert   "Greening the Ghetto: Can a Remedy Serve for Both Global Warming and Poverty?" *New Yorker*, January 12, 2009. www.newyorker.com.

Terry Laudal   "The Deeper Benefits of Going Green: More than Just Buildings," GreenBiz.com, October 25, 2007. www.greenbiz.com.

Diane Mastrull   "Creating a Lasting Green Economy: Leanne Krueger-Braneky's Goal Is to Create Jobs That Pay Well and Are Long-Term," *Philadelphia Inquirer*, May 3, 2009. www.philly.com.

Sarah Max   "Your Home: Is 'Going Green' Worth the Cost?" CNNMoney.com, June 21 2007. http://money.cnn.com.

Ashley Phillips   "Will Going Green Lose Some Gusto? Environmental Concern Has Storied History of Going In and Out of Style," ABCNews.com, July 12, 2007. http://abcnews.go.com.

Jen Phillips   "China's Green Movement," *Mother Jones*, December 11, 2007. www.motherjones.com.

Pricewaterhouse-Coopers   "Green Movement Offers Significant Market Opportunities for the Technology Sector According to PricewaterhouseCoopers Study," February 13, 2008. www.pwc.com.

David Roos   "Hollywood Goes Green: Is Today's Environmental Consciousness a Trend That Will Continue?" *MovieMaker*, July 24, 2006. www.moviemaker.com.

Allyson Schwartz and Michael Nutter   "Nurturing the Green Economy," *Philadelphia Daily News*, July 7, 2009. www.philly.com.

Mark Silva   "Green Light for Environmental Movement," The Swamp (blog), April 19, 2007. www.swamppolitics.com.

John Tierney   "Use Energy, Get Rich, and Save the Planet," *New York Times*, April 20, 2009. www.nytimes.com.

UN News Centre   "'Green' Economy Vital to Promoting Development in Midst of Crises—UN Agencies," June 25, 2009. www.un.org.

Bryan Walsh   "Changing the White Face of the Green Movement," *Time*, March 23, 2008. www.time.com.

Alex Williams   "Buying into the Green Movement," *New York Times*, July 1, 2007. www.nytimes.com.

Index

A

Advertising images, 96, 102, 163–164

African Americans
economic free fall and, 78
environmental movement and, 170–171
green jobs for, 72–74
green pioneers, 169
pollution concerns and, 168

Air pollution
cap-and-trade program and, 184
contamination, 96, 187
controls, 59, 104
hydrofuel-cell, 36
improving, 104–105, 128, 169, 172–173, 196
solar paint and, 191

Air travel concerns, 54, 190

Allen, Ash, 95–107

Alliance, Apollo, 77, 78, 176

American Clean Energy and Security Act, 131

American Council for an Energy-Efficient Economy, 107

American Electric Power (AEP), 98–99, 184

American Wind Energy Association, 45

Apollo Alliance, 77, 78

Apollo's Fire: Igniting America's Clean Energy Economy (Hendricks), 79

Applebaum, Anne, 185–188

Araki, Yumi, 116–119

Archer Daniels Midland (ADM), 101–102

Arctic National Wildlife Refuge, 183

Arrowhead Mountain Spring Water Company, 84

Asia, 174, 186

Aspen Institute, 91

Associated Press, 172–174

Atkins, Stuart, 81–85

Atluru, Raj, 43, 45–46

Australia, 37, 179

B

Ball, Jeffrey, 49–52

Bank of America, 38

Barton, Joe, 98, 99, 102, 104, 107

Big Green Purse: Use Your Spending Power to Create a Cleaner, Greener World (MacEachern), 120

Big Green Purse.com, 120

Bio-mimicry science, 179

BioBased Insulation, 37

Biodiesel, 101–102

Biofuels
for air travel, 190
cost of, 110, 173
developing, 24, 72, 104
flex fuel cars and, 107
funding for, 69
harmfulness of, 101–102

Bisbee, Mark, 66

Blu Skye Consulting, 87, 88

Bond, Kit, 94

Bonney, Bob, 34

BP (British Petroleum), 103–105
Brackley, Paul, 35
Brazil, 120, 193
Bright Green Talent, 86, 88, 176
Bug Blocker Inc., 116
Bush, George W. (administration), 41, 45, 166, 183

C

California Energy Commission, 50
California Institute of Technology, 44
Calzada, Gabriel, 92, 93–94
Campbell, Karen, 149–153
Canada, 179, 180
Cap-and-trade legislation
   accounting analysis of, 152–153
   carbon tax and, 155–157
   clean energy and, 68, 184
   economic costs of, 149–151, 183–184
   emissions reduction and, 154–155
   higher taxes and, 153
Cap-and-trade system
   advantages/disadvantages of, 143–144
   benefits of, 75–77, 141–144
   cost of, 133–136
   economic growth and, 139–140
   establishing, 44, 131–132
   expected changes from, 132–134
   job loss from, 136–137
   options for, 140–141
   revenues from, 70, 71
Capitalism, 46, 74, 80
Carbon dioxide (CO$_2$)
   allowance price and, 150
   burning trash and, 102
   China and, 139–140, 189, 190
   coal economy and, 39
   electricity and, 189
   emissions, 51, 76, 108–109, 115, 131, 156
   limits on, 28
   reducing, 182
   storage of, 110
   taxing, 140–141, 184
   trapping/absorbing, 37, 189–190, 191
   See also Cap-and-trade system
Carbon tax, 155–157
Cars/vehicles
   alternative fuels for, 36, 178, 194
   biodiesel, 101–102
   electric, 113–114, 164, 190
   ethanol for, 101–102, 107
   flex fuel cars, 107
   fossil fuels and, 21, 90, 108, 182, 195
   pollution from, 56
   powering, 109
   solar powered, 165
   sport-utility vehicles, 145, 146, 147, 159
   See also Biofuels; Hybrid cars
Carson, Rachel, 20
Carter, Jimmy, 40, 45, 47
Carter, Majora, 169
Castile soap products, 122–123
Center for American Progress (CAP), 68, 71, 79
Center for Data Analysis (CDA), 151
Cheney, Dick, 41–42

China
  carbon dioxide and, 139, 140,
    189, 190
  economic expansion of, 174
  green economy and, 44
  imports from, 75
  transportation and, 190
Chu, Steven, 42, 44
Citigroup Corporation, 33–34, 38
Clarke, B. Jesse, 74–75
Clean Air Act, 20, 98, 100, 104
Clean Air Watch, 98
Clean Edge Inc., 173
Clean electricity, 189–192
Clean energy, 68, 184
Cleantech Venture Network, 173
Climate change
  developing countries and, 188
  environmentalists and, 49–50,
    193
  green building designs and,
    125–126
  green movement and, 49–52,
    79, 193–194
  legislation for, 151, 153
  technology and, 51–52
  See also Global warming
Climate Security Act, 183
Coal energy, 51, 110, 184
Compact fluorescent lights
  (CFLs), 121
Comprehensive Environmental
  Response, Compensation, and
  Liability Act (CERCLA), 105
Congressional Budget Office
  (CBO)
  cap-and-trade legislation and,
    76, 131–137, 149–153
  carbon dioxide (CO_2) and,
    150
  energy costs and, 151–152

Corporate green practices
  business/supplier relation-
    ships, 37–38, 58
  day-to-day operations, 35–36
  financial incentives for, 32–33
  green offices and, 129
  pollution from, 95–107
  products/technology, 36–37
  in workplaces, 33–34
  See also Green economy/
    business
CorpWatch, 103–104
Cosmeticsdatabase.com, 122
The Cost of Green Revisited
  (Langdon), 126
Crawford, Jennifer, 124–130
"Creation Care" environmentalism, 160
Cuddeback, Craig, 173

D

DaimlerChrysler, 107
Danaher, Kevin, 62, 63
Davis Langdon (construction
  consultants), 126
DeAngelis, Lauren, 145–148
DeCicco, John, 52
Defense Advanced Research
  Projects Agency (DARPA), 46–47
Delhi Auto Expo, 185
Deloitte Consulting LLP, 32
Denmark, 46
Denver Post (newspaper), 155
Department of Energy (DOE), 42,
  43, 46, 47, 183
Department of the Interior, 20
Department of Transportation
  (DOT), 114

Designing the Green Economy (Milani), 75
Dichlorodiphenyltrichloroethane (DDT), 20
Dickson, Joe, 121
Dikeman, Neal, 138–144
Dirty Dozen, 98, 99, 102, 103–104, 107
Doerr, John, 172–173, 174
Douglas, Karen, 50
Dow BioProducts, 37
Dow Chemical, 105–106
Draper Fisher Jurvetson, 43
DuPont company, 100

E

Earth Day, 20
Earth First!, 21
Earth Institute, 180
Earth Liberation Front (ELF), 21
Eco-Cement, 37
Eco-Green Living, 61
Eco-Homes, 24
Eco Taj policy, 35
Ecomagination program, 63, 64
Economy
    cap-and-trade system and, 134, 139–140
    environmental movement and, 21, 109, 185–188
    green jobs and, 176–177
    green movement and, 79–80, 185–188
    green products and, 118–119
    low-carbon, 189–192
    re-engineering global energy and, 110–111
    restructuring, 21
    See also Green economy/ business

Education in sustainability, 179–180
Electric vehicles, 113–114, 164, 190
Electricity. *See* Clean electricity
Ella Baker Center for Human Rights, 77
Ellis, Nick, 176
Endangered Species Act, 20, 159
Energy-efficient innovations, 117–118, 135
Energy Information Administration (EIA), 108–109
Energy Star program, 33, 117
Environment Program, (UNEP), 176
Environmental Defense Fund (EDF), 51, 52, 108, 109
Environmental fraud, 103
Environmental Protection Agency (EPA)
    African Americans and, 169
    cap-and-trade legislation and, 153
    carbon dioxide and, 109
    Clean Air Act violations and, 98, 100, 104
    Dow Chemical *vs.*, 105, 106
    electric cars and, 113
    Energy Star program and, 33, 117
    establishment of, 20
    greenwashing and, 97
    hybrid cars and, 145
    regulation by, 141
Environmentalists/environmental movement
    changes in, 170–171
    climate change and, 49–50, 193
    concerns of, 21

corporations and, 95
economy and, 21, 109, 185–188
global warming dangers and, 111
green pioneers, 169
racism and, 79
religious groups as, 159–161
sustainability and, 28
urban quality and, 72
Ethanol, 101–102, 107
Europe, 45–46, 49, 50, 139, 155
European Union, 37, 92
Exxon Valdez oil spill, 20, 99
ExxonMobil, 99–100
Ezdiyelectricity.com, 118

F

Feldstein, Martin, 156
Finland, 37, 56
Flaherty, Pamela, 33–34, 38
Flame Engineering, 116
Flex fuel cars, 107
Food and Agriculture Organization (FAO), 178
Forbes (magazine), 179
Ford Escape Hybrid (car), 146
Forest Stewardship Council, 120
Fossil fuels, 21, 90, 108, 182, 195
Freilla, Omar, 79
Friedman, Thomas L., 36
Friends of the Earth, 53, 54

G

General Electric Co. (GE), 62, 63, 66, 97–98
General Motors (GM), 98, 106–107, 113–115, 146

Geothermal power, 21, 24, 25, 177, 182, 184, 195
Germany, 21, 28
Gestrich, Thomas E., 103
Gibbs, Robert, 93
Giddens, Anthony, 53–56
Giuliani, Rudy, 169
Global energy systems, 108–111
Global Exchange, 62
Global positioning system (GPS), 47, 65
Global warming
dangers of, 111, 128
deniers, 99
legislation and, 104
pollution and, 101
transportation industry and, 113–115, 125
See also Climate change
Goldman, Arnold, 45
Google Inc., 172
Gore, Al, 21, 27, 39, 45, 162, 186
Government spending, 70–71
Graves, Sam, 102
Green, Joshua, 39–48
Green Building Council, 23, 34, 180
Green building designs
benefits of, 127–129
climate change and, 125–126
cost of, 126–127
for existing buildings, 129–130
jobs and, 177–178
soybean-based foam insulation for, 37
strawboard manufacturing for, 37
structural insulated panels and, 25
triple-glazed windows, 191

See also Leadership in Energy and Environmental Design

The Green Collar Economy (Jones), 165–166, 169

Green Drinks, 181

Green economy/business
  awareness of, 41–42
  barriers to, 86–88
  competition and, 63–64
  green jobs and, 67–71, 88–90, 176–177
  growth of, 62–63
  market diversity and, 64–66
  Obama, Barack and, 43–44
  overview, 39–41
  poverty and, 72–80
  supplier relationships, 37–38, 58
  technological advances in, 44–48, 172–174
  See also Corporate green practices

Green Festival, 61, 74

Green for All, 77, 176

Green Globes, 125

Green Home company, 117

Green jobs
  for African Americans, 72–74
  in building industry, 177–178
  carbon caps and, 75–77
  careers and, 178–180
  creating, 67–71, 77–79
  defined, 175–176
  economy and, 67–71, 88–90, 176–177
  expense of, 92–94
  greenwashing of, 175
  opportunities for, 180–181
  politicians and, 18
  training for, 88–90
  transformation needed, 74–75
  unproductiveness of, 93–94

Green Jobs Act, 75

Green Jobs Initiative, 176

Green marketing, 81–85

Green movement
  climate change and, 49–52, 79, 193–194
  commitment to, 194–195
  economic issues and, 79–80
  failure risks, 166–167
  future of, 196
  ingenuity needed, 55–56
  positive images of, 164–165
  problems with, 53–55
  regulation of, 90–91
  technology and, 53–56
  vision of, 162–164

Green products
  benefits of, 35–37, 116–117, 191, 195
  carbon tax and, 140–141
  cost of, 83, 120–123
  developing, 30, 74, 81–82, 91
  economic obstacles to, 118–119, 163
  energy-efficient innovations, 117–118, 135
  exploiting nature for, 18
  increase in, 59–60, 61–66, 176–177
  marketing of, 81–85
  mass production *vs.*, 186–188
  risks with, 89, 100, 101, 103

Green Worker Cooperatives, 79

GreenBiz.com, 179

Greenercars.org, 107

GreenFloors, 66

Greenhouse gas (GHG) emissions
  biofuels and, 101–102
  brokers for, 179
  building industry and, 124
  coal and, 51
  ethanol and, 101–102

green economy and, 177
Kyoto Protocol and, 45, 90
regulation of, 141
See also Carbon dioxide (CO₂)
Greenhouse gas (GHG) emissions,
  reducing
  business relationships and,
    37–38, 58
  compliance with, 50
  cost of, 75–76, 131, 135–136,
    139
  strategies for, 125
  vehicles for, 194
  from workplaces, 33
  See also Cap-and-trade system
Greenpeace, 54, 104
Greensburg, Kansas, 23–26
Greenwashing, 89–90, 95, 97–98,
  175
Gross domestic product (GDP),
  71, 138, 139, 149, 151
Guardian (newspaper), 99

H

Habitat for Humanity, 121
Hannam, Paul, 86–91
Hansen, Jim, 28
Harsanyi, David, 154–157
Haumann, Barbara, 116, 118–119
Hawkins, David, 51
Heesen, Mark, 173–174
Heino, Jan, 178
Hendricks, Bracken, 79
Heritage Foundation, 151–153
Hewlett-Packard, 60
Homeowner energy costs, 131–137
Honda (cars), 146, 147–148, 186
Honda Civic Hybrid (car), 146–
  147
Honda FCX Clarity (car), 186

House Committee on Energy and
  Commerce, 131
Hudson River cleanup, 97–98
Hybrid cars
  comparisons to, 114, 146–147
  cost of, 145–146, 186
  gas mileage from, 147–148
  transformation to, 74, 84, 95
  See also specific cars

I

Immelt, Jeffrey, 97–98
An Inconvenient Truth (Gore), 21,
  45
India
  carbon dioxide and, 189, 190
  floods in, 193
  green buildings in, 35
  green economy and, 44, 174
  Nano car impact on, 185, 186,
    188
Indonesia, 103
Industrial pollution, 168
Industrialism, 54
Inhofe, Jim, 98, 103
Insulating concrete forms (ICFs),
  25
Intergovernmental Panel on Cli-
  mate Change (IPCC), 27, 41, 186
International Paper, 102–103
Internet, 47, 190–191

J

Jackson, Lisa P., 106, 169
Jha, Alok, 189–192
Jimmy Carter Library and Mu-
  seum, 40–41
Jobs. *See* Green jobs
Jones, Van, 78, 80, 165–167, 169

K

Hurricane Katrina, 65, 168–169
Kerry, John, 168–171
Khosla, Vinod, 174
Kleiner Perkins Caulfield & Byers, 172–173, 174
Knappenberger, Chip, 153
Kreutzer, David W., 149–153
Kyoto Protocol, 45, 90

L

Landfill mining, 164
Leadership in Energy and Environmental Design (LEED) buildings
    cost of, 125–126
    education on, 180
    for existing buildings, 33, 129
    green labor and, 87
    green workplaces and, 34, 38
    in Greensburg, Kansas, 23–25
    occupancy rate of, 128
League of Conservation Voters (LCV), 98, 103
Lewis, Nathan, 44
Liberty Carpet One, 66
Light-emitting diode (LED) light bulb, 24, 117–118, 191, 195
Little, Thomas, 118
Lockwood, Charles, 32–38
Loris, Nicolas D., 149–153
Lovins, Armory, 39–40, 41, 43
Low-carbon economy, 189–192
Low-flow toilets, 121
Lyman, Zach, 65–66

M

MacEachern, Diane, 120, 121–123
Makower, Joel, 162–167, 179

Malibu Hybrid (car), 146, 147
Markey, Ed, 154–155
Marmoleum flooring, 64
Martin, Sean, 87, 88
Marx, Karl, 56
Massachusetts Institute of Technology (MIT), 110, 183
Matthiessen, Alex, 97–98
Mc-Cabe, Catherine R., 104–105
McConnell, Mitch, 102
McGraw-Hill Construction, 177
Megawatt hours (MWH), 142
Mercury Mariner Hybrid (car), 146
Merkel, Angela, 28
Michigan Department of Environmental Quality (MDEQ), 105–106
Middle East oil dependence, 40
Milani, Brian, 75
MINI Cooper (car), 147
Miscovich, Peter J., 32
Morris, Peter, 124–130
Muir, John, 19, 170–171

N

Nano (car), 185–188
National Aeronautics and Space Administration (NASA), 28, 42
National Association of Home Builders, 177
National Black Chamber of Commerce, 153
National Environmental Policy Act, 20
National Geographic Society, 19
National Park Service, 20
National Religious Partnership for the Environment, 159

National Science Foundation, 118

National Venture Capital Association, 173

National Wildlife Refuge, 183

Natural Resources Defense Council (NRDC), 51, 102

Netscape Communications Corp., 172

New Source Review (NSR), 98

New York Times (newspaper), 36, 78, 155

Newlands Reclamation Act, 19

Nguyen, Tram, 72–80

Nicholls, Mark, 38

Nike Inc., 62

Nitrogen oxide (NOx), 98

Nixon, Richard M., 183

Nobel Peace Prize, 186

Nongovernmental organizations (NGOs), 54

O

Obama, Barack (administration)
  cap-and-trade system and, 182
  on clean energy, 42, 163, 165
  green economy and, 43–46, 92, 167
  green jobs and, 21, 93, 164
  Greensburg, Kansas and, 26

O'Donnell, Frank, 98–99, 104, 106–107

Offset credits, 134

Olympic Games, 54–55

The Organic Center, 121

Organic cotton, 59

Organic Trade Association (OTA), 116, 119

Oxfam International, 54

P

Pachauri, Rajendra, 186

Palmer, Kimberly, 120–123

Pangea Organics, 65

Paul, Sunil, 47

Pelosi, Nancy, 165

People for the Ethical Treatment of Animals (PETA), 21

Perfluorooctanoic acid (PFOA), 100

Perry, Ed, 182–184

Petroleum-based products, 101–102

Pew Center on Global Climate Change, 124

Pew Forum on Religion & Public Life, 159

Pinderhughes, Raquel, 73–74

Planet Green, 26

Podesta, John, 67–71

Political Action Committee (PAC), 98, 99, 102, 103, 104, 107

Political Economy Research Institute (PERI), 68, 97, 103

Pollin, Robert, 68

Pollution concerns
  cap-and-trade system and, 182
  cleanup programs for, 105
  from corporate practices, 95–107
  from dichlorodiphenyltrichloroethane, 20
  fossil fuels, 21, 90, 108, 182
  global warming and, 101
  greenwashing, 89–90, 95, 97–98, 175
  industrial, 168
  overview, 95–96

Polychlorinated biphenyls (PCBs), 97

Polyethylene terephthalate (PET) packaging, 83
Polyvinyl chloride (PVC) packaging, 82–83
Pooh, Ellie, 61, 65
Portable document format (PDF), 83–84
Priesnitz, Wendy, 175–181
Proctor & Gamble, 60
Project Independence, 183
Propane Education & Research Council (PERC), 117
Proventia Group, 37
Public relations (PR), 60, 96, 104

R

Race, Poverty and the Environment (Clark), 74
Rainforest Action Network (RAN), 103
Reagan, Ronald, 40–41, 44, 46
Recycling efforts, 35, 38
Religious activists, 159–161, 170
Renewable energy
    availability of, 189–190, 195
    careers in, 178–179
    creating, 46
    geothermal power, 21, 24, 25, 177, 182, 184, 195
    investment in, 173
    strategies for, 69
    use of, 109
    wave energy, 104
    wind power, 69, 104, 177
    See also Solar power
Rensselaer Polytechnic Institute, 118
Reusing culture, 191–192
Reware company, 65
Riverkeeper, 97–98

Roosevelt, Theodore, 19
Rosenwald, Michael S., 61–66
Royal Society (UK), 99
Royte, Elizabeth, 102
Russert, Tim, 64

S

Saginaw Township West Michigan Park, 105–106
Samuelson, Robert J., 108–111
Saturn VUE Hybrid (car), 146
Save the Children, 54
Schwarzenegger, Arnold, 50
Science (journal), 101–102
Scott, H. Lee, 36, 58
Selin, Henrik, 117
Sequoia National Park, 19
Shekar, Preeti Mangala, 72–80
Shelton Group, 117
Sierra Club, 19
Silent Spring (Carson), 20
Singer, Stephan, 50–51
Smart Lighting Engineering Research Center, 118
Smart Mama's Green Guide (Taggart), 122
Soil depletion, 19
Solar Energy International (SEI), 180
Solar power
    for automobiles, 165
    benefits of, 115, 182
    developing, 21, 24, 40, 195
    funding for, 69, 88, 90
    green jobs and, 77, 164, 177
    growth of, 109, 173
    improving, 72, 191
    for paint, 191
    passive, 25

thermal panels, 42, 49–50, 65, 192
use of, 45, 63, 74–75, 95, 104
Soybean-based foam insulation, 37
Spain, 93
Sport-utility vehicle (SUV), 145, 146, 147, 159
Spring Ventures, 47
Staedler, Liz and Jim, 64–65
Steffen, Alex, 27–31, 193–196
Stern, Nicholas (Nick), 53, 55
Stern Report (Stern), 53
Stimulus Act, 42–43, 46–47, 75
Strawboard manufacturing, 37
Structural insulated panels (SIPs), 25
Sulfur dioxide (SO2), 98
SunPower Corp., 174
Suntech Power, 174
Superfund acts, 105, 53
Supplemental Environmental Projects (SEP), 100
Sustainable development
authority of, 27–28
changes ahead, 28, 30–31
forest management and, 178
future of, 28–30
of transportation, 178
See also Biofuels; Hybrid cars; Leadership in Energy and Environmental Design; Renewable energy; Technological advances
Sustainable South Bronx, 77
Swisher, Randy, 45

T

Taggart, Jennifer, 122–123
Tahoe Hybrid (car), 146–147
Taj Hotels, 35

Talent shortages, 89
Tax-equity gap, 43
TecEco Pty. Ltd., 37
Technological advances
climate change and, 51–52
corporate green practices and, 36–37
green economy and, 44–48, 172–174
green movement and, 53–56
Thoreau, Henry David, 18
Tidal energy, 104
Tornado-proof designs, 25
Toxics Release Inventory (TRI), 97, 102–103
Toyota Logistics Services, 34
Toyota Prius (car), 114, 146, 194
Transcendentalism, 18
Transportation industry, 113–115, 125, 187
Triple-glazed windows, 191
24/7 Wall St., 96
2008 Corporate Citizenship Report (ExxonMobil), 99–100

U

Unemployment rate, 69, 135
Union of Concerned Scientists, 107
United Kingdom (U.K.), 99
United Nations (UN), 176, 178, 186
United States (U.S.)
Department of Energy, 42, 43, 46, 183
Department of the Interior, 20
Department of Transportation, 114
Environmental Protection Agency, 20

Green Building Council, 23, 34, 180
United Technologies Corporation (UTC), 36
Urban Habitat, 78

V

Volatile organic compounds (VOCs), 34, 120
Volt (car), 113–115

W

Wal-Mart
    emissions cap by, 170
    green marketing and, 59–60, 62–64
    green programs and, 35–36, 58–59, 74–75, 179
    greenhouse emissions and, 37–38
    organic products from, 122
Walden (Thoreau), 18
Wall Street, 43, 154
Wallach, Daniel, 24
Ware, Keith, 61, 63–64

Washington Convention Center, 61
Washington Post (newspaper), 156
Waste Management, Inc., 63, 102
Wave energy, 104
Waxman, Henry, 154–155
Waxman-Markey climate change legislation, 151, 153
Whole Foods Market, 121
Wilderness Act, 20
Will, George, 92–94
Wind power, 69, 104, 177
Wood, Maggie, 121
World Business Council for Sustainable Development, 38
The World Is Flat (Friedman), 36
World War II (WWII), 20
World Wildlife Fund (WWF), 50

Y

Yosemite Park, 19

Z

Zero-VOC composite wood, 34
Zero-waste, 82–83, 84